A Devil's Ransom

Janey Clarke

First published in 2025 by Blossom Spring Publishing
A Devil's Ransom (Devil's Mountain Series) Copyright © 2025 Janey Clarke
ISBN 978-1-917938-31-0
E: admin@blossomspringpublishing.com
W: www.blossomspringpublishing.com

CHAPTER ONE

The body was found that morning.

Curly, the stable hand at Nowhere Livery Stable, was the first to open the barn. Each morning, he tended to the horses and prepared the wagon for its daily trek from Nowhere to Duloe Town.

Old Pete had been caught unawares. The blow to the back of his head had knocked him out and killed him immediately. But the killer hadn't stopped there. The death of Old Pete was tragic enough, but it was the staging of the body that caused the most uproar in Nowhere. Lying in the center of the stables, on his back, Pete held a pickaxe in one hand and a gold pan in the other. A note placed on the body read "GOLD FEVER" in large block letters, with a bag of pebbles sitting beside the old miner.

Curly backed out of the stable, his mouth forming a large silent "O" as he covered it with one hand while the other groped for the door handle behind him. Taking one last look at the sad remains of Old Pete, Curly ran as fast as he could to the sheriff's office.

"Murder! Murder!" he shouted between gasping breaths.

The door of the sheriff's office was flung open, and Lance Grey stood there, half-dressed, struggling into his shirt as he stared at the man screeching his siren call of death on the sheriff's porch.

"Who's been murdered?" By this time, the sheriff was buttoning his black shirt.

"It's Old Pete! He's lying in the stable, and it's so odd. Come and see, Sheriff. Strange business, that's what it is. Nasty to do that to a dead man." Curly muttered under his breath all the way back to the stable. His constant chattering drew looks of irritation from the sheriff, who stomped up the hill toward the livery stable. But he didn't stop Curly. He could tell the man was in shock, and if muttering made him feel better, he could mutter, thought the sheriff.

Used to death in many strange circumstances, Lance Grey, who had fought in the Civil War and was no stranger to death and killing, stared at the sight that met his eyes. Why? That was all he could think. Pete had hurt no one. Why do this to him? He glanced back at the door of the stable and saw that a crowd was gathering around the open doorway. Faces peeked in and then were pulled back as others took their place. Each wanted to see what was happening and what had happened. But most of those who saw the scene inside the stable wished they hadn't.

"It's Old Pete! It's Old Pete. Who would do that to such a nice old man?" said one man to another.

"Decent old man. Wouldn't hurt a fly," the other man replied.

"All those years up in the mountains, and he never got hurt. A couple of weeks down in Nowhere, and he lies murdered here. What is this town coming to? Who'd kill a nice old boy like that?" A large, matronly woman, arms folded, stood shaking her head at the sad state of affairs. The large voluminous apron she wore sparkled with white cleanliness in the early morning sun. Always the one to find the worst in every situation, she was relishing this.

The news spread quickly throughout the town. Old Pete had been well loved, and there was fury at the manner in which he had been treated after death. People were getting angry, and questions were being asked about how an evil murderer could stalk the streets again.

Josh was back to his routine of sleeping at the back of the general store before starting his work there. Manuel, the owner, had been delighted to see him back. Manuel was improving after his injury, allowing him to do more work. Still, it was difficult to cope with the amount of business they were getting. Prospectors high in the mountains and working the slopes of Devil's Mountain were coming into Nowhere for their shopping. The journey to Duloe Town was just too long, and every moment spent away from the digging was a moment they begrudged. Each was a moment lost from their frantic search for gold. The increasing number of gold prospectors was the reason for the increase in business, and Manuel and Eliza struggled to keep up.

Josh was horrified when he heard of Old Pete's death. He'd only met him a few times, but the eccentric old boy had been smart, clever and resourceful, and Josh had greatly admired him. It had been Old Pete who'd warned them about the dangers on Devil's Mountain, and it was his cave and hideout that had saved them from the outlaws' attempts to kill them. Josh felt he owed Old Pete a lot and knew his survival would have been in doubt without Pete's warnings and help.

But Cassidy was the one who felt the most shocked. His murder changed her life.

CHAPTER TWO

After the horrific experience they had all suffered at the hands of the outlaws on Devil's Mountain, Cassidy, and her companion Martha were staying at the hotel. Dora, the hotel owner, had welcomed them and was delighted to see them, but like everyone else in Nowhere, was caught up in the booming business was booming and had only one small room at the back of the hotel.

Reuben, Martha's new husband, had taken up his old room at the livery stable. Unable to do proper blacksmithing work because of his still-injured shoulder, he began helping with all the other tasks involved in the business. But he joined the ladies for breakfast in the hotel, as Dora always produced good food and Reuben didn't want to miss it. The three were discussing their future plans when the black-coated figure of the sheriff appeared in the doorway of the dining room. Taking his hat off, he strode into the room. After a quick look around, his eyes fixed on the three of them, and he walked over.

"Cassidy, good morning. I need to talk to you in private. Now." Without waiting for a reply, he turned and spoke to Dora. Nodding her head at his request, she led them to her office. Assured that the three were following the sheriff, she closed the door behind them and rushed to make some of the strong coffee that Sheriff Lance Grey always asked for.

Seated on the assortment of chairs Dora kept in her office, they waited impatiently to see what the sheriff wanted. But the sheriff was waiting for his coffee before he began.

The breakfast had been good, and Reuben was grateful

that the sheriff had not appeared until he had finished. However, he had felt it was a shame to leave the one remaining biscuit on the plate. Reaching for it before walking out after the others, Reuben had stuffed it into his mouth. Now, seated in the stuffy office, he was struggling to swallow it. He, too, was grateful when Dora appeared with the coffee.

Cassidy, wondering what was coming, sat struggling to remember all her misdeeds. And there were many! The petite blonde, with her dainty figure and enormous violet eyes, sat silently reviewing her past activities. Most of those she had killed had been wanted by the law, and she had amassed quite a fortune from the bounties she had collected. But she had killed no one lately.

"Cassidy, when Old Pete arrived back in town, he asked me to keep some documents and another large envelope for him in my safe. 'Not to be opened until I'm dead,' he told me. He was murdered last night."

Lance waited for their murmurs of horror to die down before continuing. "He knew you were unaware of his links with your father, Cassidy."

At Cassidy's surprised reaction, Grey nodded and continued. "They were together in the Civil War. Your father saved Pete's life, and for that, he was always grateful. But he didn't enjoy talking about the war—refused to, in fact. Unknown to you, he always kept an eye on what was happening to you. That's why he was so protective of you and Martha going up to his cave in the mountain. No one else knew about that cave or the gold he found there."

"I never knew, Sheriff. Why didn't tell me? I would have loved to hear about him and my father, and how he knew him." The shock of this news about her father had upset Cassidy, and together with the sadness at the old man's cruel death, she couldn't help but shed a tear or two. They trickled down her cheeks, and one teardrop hung from the lash of one of her brilliant violet eyes. The sheriff and Reuben, aware of the girl's beauty, were stunned into silence at how she could cry without her face and eyes becoming red and blotchy.

Coming back to the matter at hand, Grey continued. "I want you to come to the office to look at these papers and I'll hand them over to you."

"But what are these papers? What does he want me to do?" Cassidy asked, puzzled.

"Cassidy, Old Pete made you his heir. All his worldly goods are yours now. There's an envelope with your name on it. I think that'll explain everything."

The sheriff had drunk his coffee, though his face had been screwed up while doing so. Dora didn't make coffee to his liking—but it was still coffee, so he drank it anyway. Thinking of the coffeepot sitting on his stove back in the office, Lance stood and said to the three of them, "Now I've told you. Can you come back with me to check it all out?"

As he went out the door of the hotel, he was met by an angry mob. Reuben, spotting the crowd, pulled Cassidy and Martha back. "The back door," he whispered in their ears.

Cassidy, rushing down the hallway after Reuben, paused for a moment to look back at Grey standing there. Tall and commanding, she could hear his voice: "Good people, let me handle the death of Old Pete in my own way. This town is being overrun by prospectors and their wild ways. It's got to stop, so you don't need to argue with me about that. I'm going back up to the sheriff's

6

office now, and I expect some of you men in this crowd to consider this: instead of bellyaching at me, sign on as a deputy. We need more law and order in this town, but you'll have to help me. All of you." So saying, he planted his black hat back on his long black hair and walked down the porch steps of the hotel. The crowd parted, their angry comments and shouts dying away, and in the renewed silence all eyes followed Grey back to his office. Always a commanding figure, he was dressed in black, with his extra-long black overcoat billowing out behind him as he walked. He was a figure of authority.

"What will we do? What's going to happen next? If Old Pete can be murdered in such a cruel fashion, no one is safe. This town was a peaceful place before those prospectors arrived." The comments arose on all sides, each one vying for the loudest voice.

But there was the one question everyone wanted an answer to: who killed Old Pete? And why was he killed in such a weird and bizarre manner? Who was the murderer among them? What did it mean, leaving poor Pete lying dead in such a peculiar fashion?

CHAPTER THREE

The sheriff's office was small and new, having been built only a few months ago. Unfortunately, they ran out of money and had to finish it with some leftover lumber. They managed to construct a decent holding area for prisoners, but no one would pay for the iron bars. So, the jail cell remained open to the fresh air, and likely would stay that way. Reuben, the blacksmith, refused to make them without payment.

Not that any prisoners ever tried to escape—they didn't dare! Sheriff Lance Grey was a polite and well-spoken man, but deadly with his weapons. Any prisoner who thought about leaving through that open window was warned: "If you do, you'll end up in a box!"

Cassidy took the chair on the other side of the desk. The sheriff walked over, took a key from his pocket, and unlocked the safe in the corner of the room. He pulled out an envelope, which he handed to Cassidy, and a sheaf of papers, which he placed on the desk.

The envelope had only one word on it: "Cassidy". Reuben, Martha, and the sheriff watched her, hoping she would open it. Instead, she tucked it into the small bag hanging over her arm. She then looked expectantly at the sheriff—who was still hoping she'd open the envelope—and then stared pointedly at the papers on the desk.

"These are deeds to properties. Pete was a very wealthy man and owned the land and livery stable," the sheriff explained. Reuben nodded, knowing Pete had funded the livery stables on the condition that his ownership remained a secret.

The sheriff slid two more property documents to Cassidy. She glanced at them briefly and set them aside for a thorough review later. The sheriff handed her the final document with a look of interest. "This land goes up into the mountains and includes all mineral rights," he said. "Pete had started a mine up there. Part of his holdings included the cave, which now belongs to you, Cassidy."

The sheriff looked at the elegant, tiny woman sitting opposite him. Her neat costume and pretty hat made him chuckle. "Can't see you becoming a miner," he said, chuckling at the thought.

Martha opened her mouth to protest, but a kick from Cassidy's dainty shoe made her close it suddenly.

Let Lance Grey believe what he wanted, Cassidy thought. It was always better for people to underestimate her. Her delicate appearance had often led men to believe she was powerless, which had served her well while collecting bounties. Easy enough to fool a villain and shoot him dead before he realized her intentions. As Cassidy flicked through the papers under the sheriff's watchful gaze, she thought she might not need to bounty hunt any more. Maybe, just maybe, Pete had made her a wealthy woman.

**

Meanwhile, Josh had been helping Manuel out for just a day in the general store, and couldn't continue. There were too many unanswered questions, especially now that his brother was dead. Josh had been found unconscious and without memory in the desert some time ago. Various attempts on his life had been thwarted, but he hadn't known who his assassin was until a few days ago. Horrified to discover that the man wishing him dead was his younger brother, Josh was desperate for answers. With his brother's death, he was still without memory and without answers.

"Manuel, I know you're busy, but I have to find out about my brother. The sheriff is searching for his hideout in the mountains today. I have to go with him. There might be something there that can tell me more about my past."

The large shopkeeper stared at the young man before him. Josh had been pistol-whipped across the face, and his broken nose was still swollen and bruised. His eyes held a haunted, lost look. Manuel, a large Mexican who enjoyed his food and drink, hitched up his trousers. Too big for a belt. He always wore braces, but they often slipped down. Manuel sighed. Josh was almost like a son, and he did not want him to leave. He relied on him for his honesty and good nature.

"You have to go, Josh. I'd want to know too. Go on, take the horse from the stable and join the sheriff."

Josh took a deep breath. He could have hugged the warm-hearted proprietor but instead murmured his thanks and dashed out the back door to the stables. As he was riding past, Eliza, Manuel's wife, rushed down the steps toward him.

"Silly man, rushing off like that," she scolded. "When Manuel told me, I couldn't believe it. Josh Barnes, come here, you need to take your stuff. You can't ride into the mountains with nothing!"

With a rueful grin, Josh dismounted and hugged the little Mexican woman. She handed him his bedroll, jacket and some food, which he stuffed into his saddlebags. "How can I thank you, Eliza? You've been so good to me," Josh said, kissing her before mounting his horse again.

Eliza watched him go. "God speed, Josh, and come

back safe to us." The tall, broad-shouldered young man, with a floppy lock of blond hair that constantly fell over his forehead, had won Eliza's heart since she first met him. Always flicking back his hair as he smiled that lopsided grin, he was a welcome addition to their household. She hoped he would return safely back to them.

Riding up to the sheriff's office, he was surprised to see several horses tied to the hitching rail. As he drew nearer, he saw the sheriff come out with Reuben, Martha, Cassidy and young Tom, the Chinese boy from Broken Horseshoe Ranch.

"Hey, Sheriff!" Josh called out. "I want to go up to the bandits' hideout, too. There might be information about my brother that can help me find out—" Josh didn't finish the sentence. There was no need; everyone knew how desperate he was to learn about his past.

"Come along, Josh. We'll be going up past the cave and then to the hideout. Went there the day before with the posse. No one there, and not much left—those bandits took everything that wasn't nailed down, so I doubt you'll find anything of use. Are you ready? We're leaving now."

CHAPTER FOUR

Before they could set off, two men raced into town.

"Sheriff! Sheriff!" They drew up in front of the group outside the sheriff's office, their horses panting, both men covered in dust from a hectic ride down from the mountain.

Cassidy watched as they jumped off their horses and ran to the sheriff, shouting, "It's war up there. There's so much fighting over claims. Look, Sheriff, we both have the same claim documents. We bought that land fair and square from that guy in Duloe. But he's a swindling crook! He's the one that's been selling it to all the prospectors up there." Both men reached the sheriff and waved pieces of paper in his face.

"Let me see them," said Grey, reaching for the papers. Reading one and then the other, he placed them side by side, gave a nod of his head, and passed them back to Cassidy.

"Yeah, both the same claims. Reckon you've both been fooled. Some guy's been selling false claims. Has this happened to others up there?" He jerked his head toward the mountain, and everyone knew what he meant.

"Yes, Sheriff. You'd better get up there as soon as possible. Somebody is going to get killed for sure," one man said, nodding to the other.

The tall, rangy one with the grubby overalls turned back to his horse. Cassidy saw it had a bedroll, saddlebags and basic mining tools strung on it. "I've had it. There's no gold up there, and even if you find it, you can't prove it's yours with a false bill of sale to your claim. I'm off to the other gold field that's opened up further west. They're finding nuggets there."

"I'm going with him," the short, dumpy one said. "Gonna be trouble up there on Devil's Mountain. Best get out of it and head to another gold field where there aren't so many prospectors."

"Yes," muttered the tall one. "Gonna get something to eat before we head off." With a nod at Grey, he took his horse and led it up the street, his friend following beside him. They had a spade, a small pick, and a pan with their bedrolls. That was all they needed to start fresh on another gold field.

Cassidy watched them. They were dispirited, but she could see that they were not without hope. They were convinced that one day they would strike it rich. That giant nugget would be in their hands; it was only a matter of time. They were sure of it. They had gold fever!

"Yet another reason for me to go up to Devil's Mountain," said Grey. As they all turned their horses toward the hills, he gave a dry laugh. "I thought clearing the bandits out would give me peace and quiet on Devil's Mountain. I should have left those rogues there. Maybe they would have rid me of the miners."

The morning had gone by the time they reached the cave where Reuben and Martha had originally set up camp. Cassidy remembered how happy they had been and how hopeful they were of finding gold and making a successful trip to the mountains. But that had all changed. First Reuben became injured and hurt his arm, then the bandits raided them, destroying everything. They narrowly escaped with their lives. But now they were going back up there. Neither was certain they would stay, and nor were they sure they would enjoy living back there. But they had left valuable goods behind. Hoping no thieves had looted their camp, they were going up.

"It all looks the same down here, doesn't it?" Martha said as they paused, looking around. The narrow, treacherous cliff-side path leading up to the cave was in front of them. Reuben led the way. His sure-footed horse was familiar with the journey and knew the treacherous parts of the path where it needed to slow down and take its time. Martha followed him, and the others soon appeared in the clearing at the top of the path.

"No one discovered the cave," Martha shouted from behind the rocks. "Everything is here just as we left it." She emerged from the darkness of the cave with an armful of supplies to make lunch.

Grey looked at the bundle in her arms and let out a heavy sigh. "I haven't got time. I have to work and get up to the mountain—first to the diggings, then to the robber's hideout."

"Nonsense!" Martha said. "Eat a meal with us now, and that will save you time later. You won't need to bother." Efficient as always, she lit a fire, and soon biscuits were cooking alongside bacon and the fresh bread brought from the hotel that morning.

Everyone noticed Grey's eyes fixed on the food Martha was producing, but it was the bacon smell, Cassidy thought, that swayed him. With a dramatic sigh, he sat himself down and accepted a cup of coffee.

"To your liking, Sheriff?" Martha asked, watching his face.

"No one makes coffee just right," Grey said before sipping it. Prepared to hide his disappointment, he stopped after the sip, then took another, this time a much bigger one, almost a gulp. "It's good, Martha. You're the only other person in Nowhere who can make a decent cup of coffee. This was worth staying for, never mind the food."

The others laughed as they all sat around the campfire, eating and drinking. The meal was eaten quickly. No one wanted to linger. Cassidy, Josh, Grey and young Tom were making their way up Devil's Mountain. To reach the bandits' hideout, they had to ride through the diggings, the area alongside the creek where most of the prospectors were living and working.

What were they going to find up there? The information from the two miners meant that there could be troublesome problems the sheriff had to face. If fighting had broken out among the miners, Grey was worried that he couldn't handle it on his own. The men in Nowhere had rallied round to make up his posse to attack the bandits and rid the mountain of their presence for good. This was different. Most of the miners were hardworking souls who had left everything behind in the desperate search for gold. Eager to make a new start in life, their motives would be understood by the people of Nowhere. There would be sympathy for them. No one would want to go up there and have a shoot-out with them. Sheriff Lance Grey realized he had a hard task in front of him.

Cassidy, meanwhile, was also worried about what they would find up at the creek diggings. The fraudulent documents giving the miners false claims were from some villain pretending to own the land. And Cassidy had just found out that the land on which the miners were digging belonged to her!

CHAPTER FIVE

The journey up to the diggings was ridden in silence. No one spoke. Grey wondered what he might face and how, being a lawman, he would be received by the rough miners. Josh wasn't even thinking about the diggings. His mind was focused on what he would find at the ransacked robbers' camp. As for Tom, the inscrutable face of the young Chinese gave little away, but he was enjoying the outing away from the routine of the Broken Horseshoe Ranch.

The noise was heard first while they were still some way away. The clinking of metal on stone, the flowing of water, shouts, and constant hammering and banging. They came to the top of the ridge and looked down on the scene of chaotic, industrious activity. Makeshift tents and rough-hewn wooden shanties lined the banks of the creeks. This had become a transient village, buzzing with life from dawn to dusk. The onlookers could see miners' equipment strewn about: pickaxes, shovels, pans and sluice boxes, all showing signs of heavy use.

Some miners were panning for gold in the shallow waters of the creek, swilling their pans with precision and watching for the telltale glint of gold dust or gold nuggets. Others were digging into the creek banks or the hillside, shovelling rocks and soil into wooden sluice boxes.

Tom, ever practical, watched fascinated as the sluice boxes, often set at sloped angles to let the water flow through, washed away the lighter soil and gravel, leaving behind the heavier particles, hopefully of gold.

Cassidy was intrigued by the miners' peculiar attire. Their practical, often tattered clothing included wide-brimmed hats to shield them from the relentless sun. Their flannel shirts and sturdy trousers were caked with mud, especially their boots.

None of the miners bothered with the newcomers. They were too focused on finding the elusive gold.

The group rode down to the diggings. As they approached, a man of gigantic proportions rose from the creek. He held a pan in his meaty hand and looked straight at them. Handing the pan to the man working beside him, his eyes, like the hard rock he was digging into, scrutinized each newcomer.

"What do you want?" The voice was loud, and those nearby paused in their activity to look up.

"I'm Sheriff Lance Grey of Nowhere Town. There's been talk of miners being sold fraudulent claims, and I've come up to see what it's about."

The giant nodded, then gestured to the others. "What about them? What are they doing here? Especially a woman."

Josh answered, "I've come up to look for the robbers' hideout. My brother was up there, and I wanted to see if there was anything of his left behind."

Cassidy was impressed by this remark. It was straightforward and kept everything secret.

The giant nodded again, then pointed directly at Cassidy. "What's she doing up here? We don't want no women here. This is a strange land. These are haunted mountains and women are not wanted."

Eager to stand up for herself, Cassidy knew this time it would not be wise. If ever a man disliked or feared women, this giant was undoubtedly one of them. There was a brief silence, as no one knew how to answer.

Again, Josh spoke up. "She's my sister. She wants to

see where our brother died and say a prayer for him." Josh thought it was the best he could do on short notice and wondered if it would be accepted by this giant of a man.

Cassidy tried to look suitably pious, but felt it was a losing battle. Her costume of sturdy canvas cloth with sensible boots was common enough among the women of Nowhere. But Cassidy had added the tiny buttons she so loved on her costume's front and sleeves. Its style and cut made it stand out from the ordinary. Her hat protected her from the sun, but the delicate frills and decorative ribbons showcased her unique style and bold personality, which was uncommon in the gold fields.

The giant accepted this and stood back. Then he shouted, his massive chest expanding, and his voice echoed across the diggings. "Let them pass! Leave them be as they travel through the diggings!"

With a nod of thanks to the man, Grey led the way, Cassidy close behind him. Josh and Tom followed. They picked their way through trenches, potholes and tools piled high beside ground littered with tailings of mud and gravel that had been sorted through and found useless.

Josh wondered if anyone had indeed found gold there, but he knew better than to ask. They rode on. Each kept a hand ready to draw a gun and fight for their lives. It would have been useless. The sheer number of miners would have immediately overwhelmed them, which could have been quite disastrous. Thankfully, none wished to spare the time away from their gold digging to question their presence further.

They rode on for some time, further up the canyon. All remembered the frantic struggle and terror they had felt only a short time ago as they sought to free the prisoners from the bandits.

"The clifftop dwellings look exactly the same. For so many years they have been up there, and there they stay, watching and watching," Cassidy said, the violet in her eyes verging on black as she remembered the horrible events that had occurred up there among the Indians and themselves.

"Do you want to camp now? There's a likely spot over there. Or would you rather wait till we reach the camp itself?" Grey asked the group as he came to a halt beside the small stream that led into the larger creek beside the miners' diggings.

"Not the camp, not where those villains stayed hidden away from the law. I don't want to stay there," Cassidy blurted out.

Tom, the young Chinese who rarely spoke at all, suddenly surprised them all by saying emphatically, "We must not stay there. That would be bad for us. This is a good place. We camp here for the night."

CHAPTER SIX

The lawman kept looking behind them.

"Do you think we were followed?" Josh asked.

"Maybe. Those men are desperate. Our horses and guns would sell for a good price and give them a fresh start. I'm worried about that. But I think the real problem will be when we return this way. It would be easy enough to lie in wait for us on our way back down." Grey stood for a moment, looking around the small clearing. "Let's take no chances. One of us will stay on watch all night, and we'll put the horses over there while we lie up with our backs against the ridge. A fire to brew coffee, then we put it out."

Both Josh and Cassidy smiled as they got busy. No matter what was happening, Grey had to have his coffee.

***

When it grew dark, they took turns keeping watch throughout the night. Restless, they all listened for any stealthy approaches.

"There was nothing that night, but I think you may be right, Grey," Cassidy said thoughtfully as they prepared to ride off. "It would be easy enough to lie in wait for our return, and we may well have found objects of value. I suggest we go up over the ridge behind the clifftop dwellings and back down toward Broken Horseshoe Ranch. Do you remember the way, Josh?"

"Not really, but remember, my face was in a bad way, and I could hardly see where we were going after the beating I had." Josh shuddered, remembering the shoot-out and the violent ending on their last visit to the bandits' hideout.

"I remember the way," said Tom. "I can guide us back down."

"Good. Maybe I could have managed it, but I wasn't sure." Cassidy smiled at Tom. "I forgot, you have a great memory."

A smile crossed Tom's normally solemn face. He finally felt like a valued member of the group.

The approach to the robbers' hideout was difficult because of the terrain, but also because of the feelings it aroused in all of them. None of them could remember that night without horror and fear sweeping over them.

Then Grey began speaking: "I don't know what happened up here. When I got here, all the action was over. I just had to arrest the villains, patch up those that were wounded and bury the dead. What went on up here?" Lance looked from one to the other. He knew all three of them had been present when the attack on the bandits' hideout had taken place.

None of them answered him. He shrugged his shoulders, sighed, and rode forward in front of them. They rode behind him, still silent, still deep in thoughts of that night. Not one of them wished to discuss the ordeal that they had lived through.

The debris from the explosions still littered the ground. The wooden hut that had been the gang's headquarters had its door hanging off. Wreckage lay everywhere: implements broken and twisted in the blast, torn pieces of clothing left, and the tent coverings split and singed by fire. Cassidy walked among it, her nose screwed up in distaste at the smell that still hung around the place.

"Still a terrible place. The wicked men have left, but the evil stays here," Tom muttered.

Josh's quick steps toward the hut showed his eagerness to find something. Anything to help him in his quest for his past life. He yanked the door off its remaining hinge. He had to get past it to step into the hut, which had been one of the hiding places for his brother, Duke. Surprisingly, there was little damage inside. A table cobbled together with bits of wood was against one wall. A bed lay undisturbed against another wall. Any items of value had been removed. Nevertheless, Josh looked around, unwilling to give up hope. Dropping to his knees beside the bed, he pulled it away from the wall, hoping something would have been hidden there. Nothing. A footstep behind him made him whirl around. "Cassidy, you startled me," he confessed, ashamed of being so jumpy, and began pulling the bed apart. Nothing. He sat back on his heels and stared at her.

Cassidy was standing in the middle of the room. Methodically, she searched one wall, then the other, and then she began looking at the floor. Most timber huts were hastily constructed and had only dirt floors, but this one had a wooden floor. Cassidy's eyes widened, and she took a step toward Josh. "Move the bed, Josh. Look in the corner beneath it. Those planks of wood, they look different from the others."

Josh jumped to his feet and flung the bed to one side as quickly as he could. He dashed back to join Cassidy, who was on her knees, looking intently at the wooden planks. "Just there," she pointed.

It took a moment before his eyes focused on the darker marks on one plank. With difficulty, he stared again, then stretched out a finger to the plank where the grease marks of fingers could be seen—only possible if you knew where to look. Otherwise, they would not have been noticed. He glanced at Cassidy, who smiled at him and nodded. "Go on, Josh. Press the wood."

CHAPTER SEVEN

It took some pushing, but when the plank shifted, it became easy to pull out. It had been cut smaller than the rest of the floorboards. Peering into the gap, all they could see was dirt beneath. Josh thrust his hand in and began feeling around. At first, there was nothing, and Cassidy saw the disappointment sweep over his face. Shifting himself, he lay almost flat and reached in further.

Cassidy observed him become rigid, and then he softly murmured, "There's something here. Just a bit further. I have it." His hand emerged from the gap, clutching a small leather case. Twisting around, he sat with it between them. Josh looked down at it.

"Open it, Josh. Hurry up. Open it!" Cassidy's voice grew shrill with excitement.

A waxed cord was wrapped around the case, and Josh untied it with trembling hands. Inside were some documents. One bore the name of the boarding house in Duloe. Another was a receipt for long-term lodgings for a child and tutor at the same boarding house. As Josh read each piece of paper, his puzzlement grew. He passed them to Cassidy. The last paper was a birth certificate for a child born in England.

"What do these mean? What child?" Josh's confusion was evident in his voice.

Cassidy read them again, then rose to her feet. She brushed down her clothes and stood for a moment with the papers in hand. "These are important documents. Otherwise, they wouldn't have been hidden here. Josh, check again to make sure there's nothing else. He might have pushed something else in quite a way back, knowing their camp was being attacked."

"Yes, I'd better make sure there's nothing else there." Josh removed another plank beside the one he'd already pulled up, widening the gap in the floor.

Lying flat again, Josh spread his arms in all directions. Just as he was about to give up, he felt something else. "There's something here." Pulling a burlap bag from the hole, he placed it on the floor. "It's heavy." As he loosened the cord, the bag fell open, revealing gold nuggets.

"Gold. It's gold nuggets. Duke must've hidden them away, along with the documents."

Josh rose to his feet after tightening the cord. "It was well worth coming here, but it doesn't give me any more answers. Only more questions."

Together, they walked out of the hut to find the others slowly returning from their searches around the camp. Tom was carrying a pistol and a rifle. "This was hidden at the back of a tent. The looters must've missed it when they came through."

Lance looked at them all. "I found nothing. But you two look like you've been successful. What have you got there?"

Josh showed the document case and turned to Cassidy, who had been carrying the gold. To his astonishment, she shook her head and patted the canvas bag she was carrying. Cassidy thought they should keep it hidden from the others, Josh thought. If the sheriff knew about it, perhaps he would take it as evidence or something. Yes, perhaps Cassidy had been wise in hiding it away.

The objects they found were shown and discussed, but Grey hurried them along, frequently glancing behind them.

"My gut says we have to move. Now! I think some

men from that mining camp are after us. Come on, Tom, let's test your memory and see how far we can get down the other side of the ridge. I won't rest easy till we reach Broken Horseshoe Ranch. I wonder if there have been rumors of that gold treasure hidden in the village. That would be something for them. Let's go."

Soon they were riding along in front of the clifftop dwellings. They passed the spot where the young Indian had fallen to his death. The scars from the explosions that had saved them were visible on the cliff face, jagged marks left by Tom's dynamite. "That dynamite was powerful." Tom looked up with pride at the damage he had caused. They rode on and up toward the ridge and had almost reached the top when they paused. Lance looked back down at the camp, now some distance below. "Look, I see riders there. I told you. My gut is never wrong."

Sheriff Lance Grey, or rather his gut, had been correct. Three riders were cautiously approaching the camp.

"Hurry, the sooner we get over this ridge, the less chance they have of seeing us," Grey said, urging them all forward.

The escape from the bandits' hideout was executed with extreme caution. Speed was crucial, yet they also had to avoid the risks of falling rocks, whinnying horses, or any movement that could be spotted by those below. Their eyes constantly flicked back to the three men searching through the debris and around the rocks for them.

Once they descended over the ridge, they could finally relax, though they felt the need to maintain their speed in case they were being followed.

"I never want to come up this hill again," said

Cassidy. "There always seems to be trouble here. Now I understand why they call it Devil's Mountain."

"There seems to be a lot of death around it. And now we have the miners in that camp causing trouble, "Grey said with a frown, revealing his concern about the miners' potential for causing him yet more problems. "Yes, it's truly a Devil's Mountain!"

CHAPTER EIGHT

Josh rode as if in a dream, his mind racing to process the information he had discovered. When Grey had caught up with them, Josh had shared only the bare minimum of details from the document case. He had been about to mention the bag of gold when he noticed it was missing.

The nudge on his ankle made him look up at Cassidy. She patted her bag and smiled at him, then casually put a finger to her lips and patted the bag again. Understanding her message, Josh decided not to tell Grey about the gold and instead continued talking about needing to visit Duloe.

"So, you think this child is still there in Duloe Town?" Grey asked as they rode toward Broken Horseshoe Ranch.

"Looks like it, if these papers are right. I need to go to Duloe next," Josh replied, a worried look on his face.

Seeing Josh's expression, Cassidy knew exactly what he was thinking. "Don't worry, Josh. I'll come with you. I can see you're worried about handling a child."

"Would you, Cassidy? You're right, I don't know what to do around children. Thanks."

"Can I come with you?" Tom asked unexpectedly. He looked from one to the other, his usually calm face now excited. "I can help with the horses. I can cook."

Cassidy looked at him and laughed at the eager face of the young Chinese boy. "Tom, I don't mind you coming, but why would you want to?"

"I like it on the ranch, but I like doing things away from the ranch," Tom said, struggling with the right words but conveying his enjoyment of the new and interesting situations they were finding themselves in.

"Reckon you were bored on the ranch," Grey said,

laughing. "The boy wants to see something of the world, something interesting."

Both Tom and Cassidy found the narrow trails back down to Broken Horseshoe Ranch.

It had been a long, dusty and tiring day. They willingly agreed to spend the night and enjoyed the company of Nancy, Ezra, and Leah.

Tom had some explaining to do to his younger brother, Chan. Unable to understand his older brother's sudden restlessness, Chan tried to persuade him to stay at the ranch. "We've traveled enough, brother. First all the way from China to America. That was a terrible journey, and we saw how happy we could be if we settled in a spot with good people. Then you traveled across half of America to reach me. Wasn't that enough traveling and excitement for you, Tom? Why don't you want to stay at the ranch? I thought living at Dry Creek Ranch would be change enough for you."

Tom stood helplessly under his younger brother's protests. He couldn't explain it himself. All he knew was that he enjoyed the excitement of being with Cassidy and Josh. "Sure, Chan, it's dangerous, but I felt I needed something other than looking at a cooking stove."

"But you can do all the digging in the garden if you'd rather do that," Chan replied, puzzled as everyone laughed.

"Good choice there, Tom," Ezra said, laughing. "Digging or cooking, not much of a choice."

"Leave the boy be. Let him travel around a bit. He'll soon want the security of life on the ranch," Grey said. "If you're coming with us, Tom, let's get some sleep. We're leaving early. I need to get back to Nowhere Town and see what's happened in my absence with those miners."

***

The next morning, Cassidy, Tom, Josh and Sheriff Lance Grey left Broken Horseshoe Ranch early, riding toward Nowhere Town. As they approached the outskirts, they could see the once-quiet town now teeming with activity. Tents and makeshift shacks spread out in all directions, and the sound of hammers, voices and the occasional gunshot filled the air.

"Looks like the place has grown a lot since we were last here," Grey said, his eyes scanning the chaotic scene.

"It's like a different town," Cassidy replied, noting the number of prospectors and miners milling about.

They rode into the town's main street, dust kicking up around their horses' hooves. In the center of the bustling street, a new large tent with a sign reading "Golden Nugget Saloon" stood prominently. Men crowded around it, some stumbling drunk, others engaged in loud conversations.

Josh's eyes narrowed as he spotted a group of rough-looking men arguing near the saloon. "This could get ugly," he muttered.

As they dismounted and tied their horses, a sudden shout erupted from the crowd near the saloon. Two burly miners, both reeking of alcohol, were squaring off, fists raised.

"Get outta my way, you no-good claim jumper!" one yelled.

"Not until you pay me what you owe, you thief!" the other shot back.

Before anyone could react, the two men lunged at each other, throwing wild punches. The crowd quickly formed a circle around them, cheering and jeering.

"Stay back," Grey ordered, pushing through the crowd

with Cassidy, Josh and Tom close behind. "Break it up, you two!"

But the fight only escalated. The men crashed into a table, sending bottles and glasses flying. One miner pulled out a knife, and the other grabbed a broken bottle.

"This is bad," Cassidy said, her hand hovering near her revolver.

Grey stepped forward, drawing his gun and firing a shot into the air. "I said break it up!" he shouted.

The crowd fell silent, and the two men froze, their weapons still poised. Slowly, they backed away from each other, breathing heavily.

"Now, drop your weapons," Grey commanded. Reluctantly, the men obeyed.

Josh took a deep breath. "That was close."

Cassidy nodded. "Too close."

Suddenly, a shot rang out from behind them. They spun around to see another group of miners rushing toward them, led by a tall, menacing man with a scar across his cheek.

"Looks like we've got more trouble," Tom said, his hand on his holster.

The scar-faced man sneered. "This town ain't big enough for the likes of you lawmen. We got our own rules here now."

Grey stood his ground. "Not while I'm around. If you don't want to end up like those two, you'll stand down."

The man laughed harshly. "We'll see about that." He drew his gun, and his men followed suit.

In a split second, Cassidy, Josh and Tom drew their weapons, forming a tight circle with Grey. The tension was palpable, the crowd around them holding their breath.

CHAPTER NINE

The scar-faced man fired, the bullet whizzing past Grey's ear. Instantly, the air was filled with gunfire. Cassidy shot one attacker in the leg, causing him to drop his gun with a howl. Josh aimed carefully and disarmed another, while Tom knocked a miner out cold with the butt of his revolver.

Grey and the scar-faced man exchanged shots, the sheriff's movements swift and precise. Finally, Grey's bullet found its mark, hitting the man's shoulder and sending him sprawling to the ground.

"Anyone else?" Grey asked, his voice calm but authoritative.

The remaining miners backed away, their eyes wide with fear. The crowd dispersed, murmuring among themselves.

Cassidy holstered her gun, her eyes scanning the now-quiet street. "Well, that was exciting," she said with a wry smile.

Grey nodded. "Too exciting. We need to find out who's stirring up all this trouble."

Josh stepped forward. "Let's start with the saloon. Someone in there must know what's going on."

Together, they walked into Golden Nugget Saloon, determined to uncover the source of the town's newfound chaos and to restore some semblance of order to Nowhere.

No one knew anything. If they did, they weren't discussing it with the lawman. Surveying the hastily erected tent saloon, they were amazed at how swiftly the owner had thrown together a saloon that could have graced any town.

"Who owns this place? I want to speak to the owner,"

Grey said to the barmen. Two men stood serving drinks. Both large men had been in more than one fight, and Cassidy noticed the two large clubs carefully placed behind them, within easy reach. "When did this saloon go up?"

"Three days ago. I brought everything in wagons from my last place. That was a town that had gold fever, but the gold ran out. I'm here for as long as the gold is here." The voice came from behind them.

On turning, they were speechless at the sight of the woman approaching them. A large woman, she would have made an excellent wrestler. Dressed in purple satin with an elaborate hairdo of curls piled up upon her head, with matching purple braids and bows. The material of her dress strained and pulled over her ample figure.

Each one of them was given a careful, searching look. Her gaze rested finally on Grey. She took note of his sheriff's badge. But Cassidy saw her eyes widen at the tall, dark-haired, flamboyant figure of the sheriff.

"What you want?" demanded a figure with hard, beady eyes, her face—to Cassidy's horror—artfully made-up. No decent ladies wore make-up. "I've had nothing to do with those riots. I keep a clean place, with no fights in here."

Cassidy looked at her and could see the woman would be able to not only stand her ground against many miners but could probably fell them with one blow from her powerful arms. The backup of the two heavyweight gentlemen behind the bar would also be a powerful deterrent to anyone trying to cause mischief in her saloon.

They left the saloon, taken aback by the speed of its building and the settled nature of it already in the small town. The woman had not been what they expected. Big

Lil, as she was called, had left them at a loss. Even Grey had been dumbfounded at the arrival of Big Lil and the speedy building of her saloon.

The night spent in the hotel by Cassidy was over too quickly. She luxuriated in the comfort of a proper bed with clean sheets, revelling in the ability to wash away the grime of her travels. The hardships she had endured over the past few days on her journey to Devil's Mountain had been gruelling, but she had borne them without complaint. Now, she wondered what the next few days would bring, in this wild search with Josh for his past life.

Josh had gone to sleep in the back of the general store, his usual spot when they were in Nowhere. Tom, the young boy who was growing up fast, had stayed in the hotel with Cassidy. Though small for his age, Tom's inscrutable Chinese features belied maturity beyond his years. After living in close quarters with him during the trek up and down Devil's Mountain, Cassidy had learned to read his thoughts. One thing she was certain of: he was brave and trustworthy.

"Why are you heading out so early?" Dora asked as she set down a hearty breakfast in front of Cassidy.

The hotel owner had known Cassidy and her companion Martha for some time. Martha, now married to Reuben, was still prospecting for gold up on Devil's Mountain. With Cassidy staying in the hotel on her own, Dora had taken her under her wing.

"You look exhausted, Cassidy. What exactly has been happening up on that mountain? There have been rumors, each more fanciful than the last," Dora said, sitting down beside her.

"Probably all true," Cassidy replied, biting into the

crusty bread. After days of campfire meals, the bread and butter tasted wonderful. She sipped her coffee and turned to the elderly woman beside her, whose worry was clear on her face. For so long, Cassidy and Martha had been everything to each other, with no one else in their lives. Now Martha was with Reuben, and Cassidy had an increasing number of friends, including Josh.

"It's Josh. You heard about the death of his brother," Cassidy began.

"I suspect it was by your hand, Cassidy. Your marksmanship and speed with a knife are well known to me. No one else knows how skilled you are with that knife, do they?" Dora asked quietly.

"No, they don't. It's best that they don't know. It gives me the edge when attacked."

"Does Josh know it was you who killed his brother?" Dora's words were soft. Though there were other people in the room eating breakfast, the alcove where they sat ensured their privacy. Still, Dora took no chances.

"We haven't spoken about it, but I'm pretty sure he knows. If I hadn't acted, he would be the one who is dead. His brother's gun was aimed at him, and I saw his finger tighten on the trigger. I had no choice."

"So, what now?" Dora asked, pushing the plate with the last piece of bread toward Cassidy.

"We're heading to Duloe this morning in that dreadful wagon. It's high time we had a proper stagecoach between the towns."

"Why Duloe?" Dora asked Cassidy.

Cassidy explained about the documents they had found and the child they were searching for.

"I wonder what you will find?" Dora murmured. Cassidy was wondering the same thing.

CHAPTER TEN

Despite the journey ahead of them, Cassidy was as stylishly dressed as ever. Her ensemble today was a rich wine color, with a tiny pink frill at the neckline adding the only feminine touch to the severely cut costume top and skirt, which fell almost to her ankles. Her matching wine-colored hat also featured a splash of pink, in the frill around the brim. Usually, she carried a small reticule, but today she had opted for a carpetbag instead.

Cassidy and Tom had joined Josh at the stables, where the wagon was waiting for their trip to Duloe. They climbed into the wagon and found the hard wooden seats as uncomfortable as ever. They were surprised to see they were the only occupants.

The burly wagon driver said, "No one leaving this place now. Days passed, and everyone wanted to leave. Not now. Make sure you're nice and early to come back, else you won't get a seat. People flocking in from all over the country. All sure that they'll find gold." He spat on the ground, hitched up his work trousers, put the small box they used to climb into the wagon inside, gave them a nod, and then went around to the front to climb up, ready for the journey. The three of them knew what to expect from the trip. They resigned themselves to the dust that would blow in around them, the canvas walls of the wagon doing little to keep it out. Toward midday, the canvas was too thin to stop the sun from beating down on their heads. The journey was unpleasant but had to be endured.

The noise of Duloe Town reached them long before they rode into it. A frontier town, it was the jumping-off point for many heading west. Some went further west to find that elusive better life. The town had become a melting pot of different nationalities, ages and races. Few women could be seen, and Josh and Tom were protective of Cassidy.

"Cassidy, take my arm. Watch where you're walking. It's muddy," Josh said. Despite the dry desert heat, a recent shower had left pools of muddy water. The streets of the town were nothing more than dirt paths, lined with tent dwellings and small canvas lean-tos serving as temporary homes for the newest arrivals. Some more established people had small wooden shanties, cramped and close together, making navigating the town confusing.

"It's grown since we were last here," Cassidy said. "Last time I came, I wasn't worried about being on my own with Martha. I wouldn't like it now. Thank goodness I have you, Josh and Tom, as my bodyguards."

Josh smiled down at the diminutive blonde, her violet eyes sparkling up at him with a mix of emotions and feelings. Tom, walking protectively on the other side of Cassidy, visibly swelled with pride at being called a bodyguard.

"Was this town smaller?" Tom asked as they finally reached the main street.

"Yes, it was twice the size of Nowhere, but just as quiet as Nowhere was before they discovered the gold. This"—Cassidy waved a hand at the bustling throng around them—"has happened in the past weeks, if that."

They strolled along the wooden sidewalk, recognizing familiar old stores but treading cautiously because of gaps and unevenness in certain spots.

"This is the lodging house we used before. I wonder if it's the same, with the same lady in charge," Cassidy said, pausing outside the two-storey building with the "Lodging House" sign.

She pushed open the door and walked inside, the others following. The interior looked the same, but the tables in the dining area were no longer set apart. Now, wooden tables and benches were crammed close together.

"I don't know if I've got any room left," a voice said behind them. Turning, they saw the same large woman who had been in charge of the lodging house before. No longer prim and proper, she stood in front of them with a soiled apron and hair escaping from a large bun. Her eyes were still bright, but now she had bags beneath them and a frown creased her forehead. She hurried toward them, then looked closely at Cassidy. "Oh, my dear, it's you again." She looked behind Cassidy for Martha.

"No Martha?"

"No, Martha is married now, and she and her husband are prospecting for gold. I have come here with my two friends."

The warm welcome to Cassidy extended to her friends, and even included finding a room for Josh.

"Where will he be sleeping?" the landlady asked, pointing at Tom. Cassidy was amused to see the normally inscrutable face of the young Chinese boy become even more blank as he hid his anger.

"With me. He's my friend," Josh said immediately. Cassidy looked at him in amazement. She had always known Josh to be a good guy, but the way he claimed Tom as his friend right away made her see him in a new light. As for Tom, he couldn't help it—his face broke into a smile. Cassidy thought he grew taller at that moment.

The landlady stared at Josh, first in surprise at his remark about Tom and then even more closely because of his familiar appearance. "You look like Mr. Duke," she said. "In fact, you could be related to him." This is good, thought Cassidy. If she knows Duke, our path will be easier from here on out.

"They are distant relatives, and we're looking for him. Do you know where he stays when he is in town?"

"You're looking for him?" The question was suspicious. It was obvious their landlady did not want to get into Duke's bad books by giving away information about him.

CHAPTER ELEVEN

"Yes, he has a package for me he brought from England. I've been told it's there for me to pick up," Josh said with a charming smile.

The handsome young man in front of her, with his pleasant face and charming smile, melted the landlady's heart. She found she was only too willing to give him the information he wanted.

After leaving their bags in the room, with nothing of value in them just in case someone with ill intent entered the landlady's place, they set off on their search for Duke.

"It sounds like he's staying at a hotel, not a boarding house," Josh said. "Do you know where it is, Cassidy?"

Struggling to stay together amid the jostling crowds, Cassidy shouted, "Yes, it's right at the end of Main Street, slightly uphill. It was the smartest building in town when I was last here. Everyone said the man was a fool for building a smart hotel in this place. Looking around, I'm not so sure it wasn't an excellent idea after all." As Cassidy was forcefully pushed to one side by a large matronly woman intent on shopping, she linked arms with both Tom and Josh, determined not to be knocked aside again. There was a constant bustle around them, and Cassidy was stunned to see the many stores that had sprung up as tents or wooden shanties in the short time she had been away from Duloe Town.

The crowd seemed to lessen as they moved further along, and the boardwalk was not so dirty or broken down in front of the last stores. One store served hot food and was popular; a queue had formed outside. A large sign hung outside with the word "EATS" in big letters. As they approached, the aroma of pies and coffee hit them.

They got nearer to the small queue, and Josh looked at Cassidy and Tom. "Shall we?" Both of them nodded and promptly stood at the back of the queue. Moments later, they were seated. Long tables lined either side of the tented building. Large pots on wood stoves at the back of the tent were bubbling and sizzling away. A large man stood over the pots, unmistakably the chief cook. An equally large woman stood beside him, both showing great skill and speed as food was constantly served on plate after plate. There was no choice—the plates came with beans, bacon, biscuit, mashed potatoes and onion gravy, along with a piece of beef. The three of them looked down at the plates. A few minutes later, each looked down at an individual plate exchange— exchanging the beans had been too difficult, but the biscuits and meat were easily swapped, and each had a meal they dived into with an appreciative silence.

Cassidy had noticed the crowd of people eating as soon as she entered the room. It was routine for her now to size up those who posed a threat, those who might have a weapon, and those who seemed innocuous. She was conscious of Tom beside her, stiffening as he finished his plate and put the knife and fork down. Without him noticing, she glanced sideways at him and saw his eyes were fixed on a young girl serving. Cassidy realized she had not looked at the staff of young servers. They had posed no threat to her, so she had more or less ignored them. Now she saw they were mainly young, bustling about with constant nervous looks at the cooks.

It was a young Chinese girl that Tom's eyes were fixed upon. Cassidy could see that she was so young that she was having trouble carrying the tin plates of food and was taking longer than the others to deliver them. For fear of dropping them or having the food slide off, this care was essential for the young girl. Cassidy saw she was also too thin, with a slight frame. When the meal finished, they got up to leave, but not before Tom looked back at the young girl with a worried frown on his face.

They were approaching the hotel, which had a large sign outside reading "THE DULOE HOTEL". The sign was skilfully painted and swung in the slight breeze. The hotel itself had been painted but was looking weather-beaten by the hot, dry, dusty winds and scorching sun of the desert. But it still had a prosperous look, promising luxury inside. As they approached, Cassidy noticed Tom glancing back again at the cafe they had just eaten at. With a sudden recollection, she remembered his younger brother had been forced into servitude in a kitchen and had been so clumsy he had been thrown out onto the street. Facing starvation or searching for even harder work, it had been Amy who discovered him and took him back to the Broken Horseshoe Ranch. Was Tom remembering his younger brother's experience and worrying about the young Chinese girl?

The thought was gone quickly because they were pushing open the door of the hotel. In an instant, the noise, bustle and general mayhem of Main Street were left behind. The immediate impression was one of silence. Carpet on the floor, heavy velvet drapes, and furniture padded to nearly bursting and covered with the most elaborate woven designs greeted them.

Cassidy heard Tom gasp behind her, his footsteps drawing ever closer. She could tell he was worried about being sent packing from this elite establishment, a concern she shared, as such places often had petty rules about who could enter.

Before she could speak, a woman glided up to them. Dressed in a severe black gown with a small white collar, her attire rustled as she walked. Her hair was scraped back into a tight bun, making her appear even more rigid. Cassidy remembered her mother's remark about an acquaintance being "stiff and starchy". This woman fitted that saying.

"Can I help you?" The woman's tone was polite, but her gaze, taking in their dusty, travel-stained clothes, was not. That look hoped they would turn tail and run out of the door.

Josh, who had been silent and standing behind Cassidy, stepped forward into the light of the enormous chandelier. The woman's demeanor changed abruptly. "Sorry, Duke Ravenswood, I didn't recognize you." Her voice sharpened with bewilderment as she looked more closely at him. "You look like Duke Ravenswood, but …"

Now Josh was as puzzled as she was, struggling to find words. It fell to Cassidy to sort out this confusion. "I gather Duke Ravenswood has been staying here?"

Without looking at her, the woman nodded, her gaze fixed firmly on Josh.

"This is his brother," Cassidy explained. "He's come to see him, or rather, to collect a package his brother left for him." Her words were jumbled, but she didn't want to reveal that the Duke Ravenswood they were speaking of was dead.

"I don't know about any package, but perhaps the boy's tutor could help you. Duke Ravenswood has been away on a business trip and won't be back till next week. I'll send the maid to fetch Mr. Jones." The woman walked over to a desk set against the wall in the lobby, picked up a small brass bell, and rang it. The tinkling sound echoed around the lobby and was clearly heard in the servants' quarters. A moment later, a maid, also dressed in black, rushed over.

"Yes, Mrs. Taylor," she said, looking questioningly at the three strangers.

"I'm going to show these … people into the Blue Room. Please fetch Mr. Jones immediately," Mrs. Taylor instructed. The maid bobbed her head in acknowledgment, and Cassidy marvelled at Mrs. Taylor's command over the staff.

The Blue Room was indeed very blue. Velvet drapes hung in luxurious folds, tied back with gold fabric fringed with tassels. Chairs upholstered in similar blue velvet were neatly placed around the room. The door closed behind Mrs. Taylor, and all three of them looked at the chairs but didn't sit. Even Cassidy, the tidiest and cleanest among them, knew the dust clinging to her skirt would mar the velvet.

"Duke Ravenswood? Did she mean a proper duke, like they have in England?" Tom asked Cassidy.

CHAPTER TWELVE

"That must be why he was called Duke. He just used it as his name," Cassidy replied.

"But what has this Duke got to do with me? Why was he looking to kill me? What did I ever do to him?" Josh asked, frustration in his voice.

They were so engrossed in their conversation that they didn't notice the door opening behind them. A young man, neatly dressed in a smart suit with an unusual cut, stepped into the room.

The man had been standing there for some time and had listened to their conversation. Now he spoke. "The man who styled himself as Duke Ravenswood wanted to kill you because you are his elder brother. You are the real Duke of Ravenswood." His words fell upon the silent room, and everyone stared at him, speechless. "I gather this is news to you. I recognize you from when you lived in London. Is it true you've lost your memory?"

Josh could only nod, then with effort began speaking. "I woke up in the desert with no memory of who I was. It seems I had been beaten unconscious and left to die. When I recovered, my memory did not. I have no recollection of any past life, especially not of England or London."

Mr. Jones took a deep breath. "This is very serious. I think you ought to leave immediately. If your younger brother returns, he will certainly try to kill you. Please leave at once for your own safety."

Josh looked at the young man. "No fear of that. He's been dead and buried these past three days."

There was a knock, and the door opened to reveal Mrs. Taylor. "I have brought you afternoon tea. I'm sure there is much to talk about, and tea and sandwiches may help." Two young maids followed her in, placing tea things and plates of delicately cut sandwiches and dainty cakes on a small round table. "Please, all of you, sit down. May I pour out tea for you?"

They all sat awkwardly on the beautiful velvet chairs. The maid brought each of them a cup of tea, a plate with sandwiches and a cake, setting them on small tables at their elbows. Josh took them instinctively, seemingly at ease, which Cassidy noticed with a sly smile. Tom, aware of the glances cast his way by the maids, and Mrs. Taylor relaxed at Cassidy's approving nod. If Cassidy wanted him to sit on a velvet chair and sip tea, Tom was happy to do so.

A small boy ran into the room to stare at these unknown visitors. The young man sat down opposite them, the little boy standing beside him. "You are Ravenswood. If, as you say, your brother is dead, that makes life easier for everyone." He took a large handkerchief and wiped his brow, perspiration glistening despite the cool, shaded room.

Cassidy thought it wasn't the heat making the man sweat. He was nervous, his eyes darting to the door every few moments. "How do I know that he's dead? This could be a trick," he stammered, glancing over his shoulder again.

Reaching down for the carpetbag Cassidy had been carrying, she opened it and pulled out the leather folder they had discovered in Duke's hideout. "We found this hidden away after his death. It's got documents, letters to this place, and the birth certificate of a boy named Charles."

Taking the folder from her hand, he inspected the

contents and then sat back in his chair. An expression of relief mingled with apprehension crossed his face.

"Can I go back to the kitchen and play with the kitten?" the boy asked, tugging at the young man's arm.

He looked down at the boy and shrugged. "There's been little for him to do here, and it kept him occupied. But he's picked up some terrible language."

"Yes, dear, you play with the kitten, and then come back and tell us all about it," Cassidy said, smiling at the little boy.

His intent gaze on her was followed by a solemn nod. He turned and walked out the door, his face and actions a mirror of Josh's, sparking a suspicion in Cassidy's mind. She turned to the young man. "He's Josh's son, isn't he?"

Josh jumped at this and stared at the young man. "My son? But—"

Before he could finish, the young man interrupted: "Have you really lost your memory?"

"Yes, I have, and now I think you'd better tell me all about the circumstances of your arrival here and all you know about this boy." Josh was getting annoyed. Here he was, finally within reach of discovering his past, and the young man was hedging around the facts without telling the truth. This was infuriating. Josh wanted to know the truth about his past life. But he was very well aware that anything he discovered would transform his present life. He liked his present life and didn't want it to change. However, he must know the truth about himself and where he came from, and what he'd done in the past.

CHAPTER THIRTEEN

After taking a sip of tea, the young man began his tale. "You were married, and your wife was expecting a baby. Your younger brother got into debt again and again— gambling, among other vices." He glanced at Cassidy, embarrassed to divulge the sordid details in front of a lady. "Your father and you helped him out repeatedly. After your father died, and when you said the estate could no longer cover his gambling debts, he took drastic action."

Another sip of tea. "You disappeared. It was said you fell off a boat while sailing on the coast. No one believed it. Everyone thought you were dead. But someone came back from America saying they had seen you. Your brother was furious, as he had given instructions for you to be thrown off a boat sailing to America. That didn't happen. Then he heard you had lost your memory after he sent men to look for you. You survived a couple of attempts on your life …"

Josh interrupted, unable to contain himself. "My wife? Who—what …"

"I'm sorry, sir. She died in childbirth. When your son was born, your brother took charge of him, controlling your estate through him. But he grew nervous at the thought of you returning from America. We came out to America some months ago." The young man drained his tea and set the cup and saucer on the table.

Silence filled the room for a long moment.

It was Cassidy who broke it. "What happens now? To the estate and to the boy?"

"There is no doubt in my mind that you are the rightful heir, the one we have been searching for. Now, I expect you to travel back with me and the boy to England to reclaim your life and your estate."

All eyes turned to Josh.

A sudden thought struck Cassidy. "We know him as Josh Barnes. Is that his real name? If not, what is it?"

The young man looked at Josh, a mixture of sympathy and expectation in his eyes. "Your real name is Joshua Ravenswood, heir to the Ravenswood estate. Josh Barnes was a name you took to keep you safe while you were here in America."

As Josh delved into the details of his heritage and life in England, Cassidy headed out of the hotel with Tom to see her lawyer. Cassidy had visited him before and had been present when he came to Nowhere to visit the Grangers. During that visit, the Grangers had signed over the deeds to their property on their ranch, and the land rising to the peak of Devil's Mountain, to Cassidy.

Cassidy had kept the ownership of the land and ranch a secret, revealing it only to Josh and Amy. Women faced difficulties in the West when it came to owning extensive properties, and she wanted to keep it confidential for the time being. What she had uncovered in Nowhere was a fraudulent scam involving land claims on her property.

Reuben, a local prospector, had been up the creek and found no gold along the land being sold as rich with gold nuggets.

"That land up there has been salted," Reuben had told Cassidy. "There is no gold in that area at all. It's further up the canyon, and around the cave."

"What is salting?" Cassidy had asked the burly blacksmith.

"It's when holes are drilled in rock and gold is planted in there. The man selling the claim goes up to that rock, smashes it open and finds gold flakes. Wouldn't you want to buy that land if you could just do that and find gold?"

Martha, a sceptical onlooker, scoffed, "Why would he be selling the land if it was so full of gold?"

"That's a good point," said Cassidy.

On the way to the lawyer's office, Cassidy explained this to Tom. "Has no one found gold up there?" Tom asked.

"No, I don't think so. I've heard that some gold has been found, but I suspect it was planted by the crook selling the land," Cassidy said.

"Selling *your* land," Tom said indignantly.

Cassidy smiled as she pushed open the door to the lawyer's office. Tom followed her in, his face becoming blank as he wondered what kind of welcome he would receive.

The lawyer rushed out to greet Cassidy, taking Tom's presence for granted. In frontier towns like Duloe, young ladies rarely walked around without a chaperone for protection. He thought Tom was there as a chaperone and bodyguard.

"Has any gold been found around Duloe?" Cassidy asked after the greetings were exchanged. "I'm certain that this prospect of finding gold up around Nowhere is a scam."

The lawyer shook his head and shuffled some papers on his desk. "Yes, there are two gold fields on the far side of Duloe. One mine has been very productive, and those working around it have made their fortune. I've heard about the scams in Nowhere. A man has been going around with maps and deeds of claims, and he looks extremely respectable and trustworthy. I have seen him in the town and complained to the sheriff, but he does nothing."

The lawyer shook his head at how the eager prospectors were being swindled. The discussion about the land and property Cassidy now owned took some time. Although Cassidy suspected the lawyer might be dragging it out to make more money, she said nothing. She was eager to learn all she could about the land she owned on Devil's Mountain, and the ongoing work on the Grangers' land was something she would have to inspect in person.

Finally, she asked the question foremost on her mind: "What about this fraudulent businessman selling the scams? What can I do about that? You know I don't want my name known as the owner of these properties. So I can't confront him in person. Can you think of any way to stop him?"

"The sheriff can't do much. He's already busy trying to keep order," the lawyer said. "Perhaps you could run him out of town?" He laughed and slapped his thigh in amusement at the idea of the petite blonde doing such a thing. He missed the look that passed between Cassidy and Tom, a look that said they thought this might be an excellent idea.

CHAPTER FOURTEEN

Tom and Cassidy left the lawyer's office.

"We'd best get the luggage we left at the lodging house," Cassidy said as they walked toward it.

"Miss Cassidy—sorry, Cassidy—staying at the lodging house is one thing. But do you really think I should stay in that hotel? It's very grand," Tom said as they approached the front sidewalk of the lodging house.

"Tom, you are staying there. You can take on the job of being my bodyguard or Josh's manservant. Would that make it easier for you?" Cassidy said, understanding his reluctance to stay there only as a companion and friend. It was unlikely anyone would understand or appreciate that.

Tom brightened. "I'll be your bodyguard. I guess going around town with you then makes sense."

Cassidy opened the door of the lodging house. The landlady had made a special effort to make them comfortable, and now Cassidy had to inform her they were leaving. But she reckoned that if she paid her, and the landlady had the rooms to sell again, she would be pleased. She was correct. The landlady pocketed the money. They collected their luggage, and left the landlady to the task of fitting in as many customers as she could.

"Miss Cassidy, do you blame me? This is my chance to make some money before I get too old to do it," the landlady had said when Cassidy paid her.

It was a sobering thought. Cassidy knew life was difficult for a single woman out West. Ensuring she had enough money for her old age was the landlady's chief aim in life.

These dismal thoughts were interrupted by Tom. "Do

you think we could run him out of town?"

Cassidy stopped dead and looked at him. A large man had to swerve swiftly to avoid her, as she stood there on the landing of the boarding house. She ignored his glare and muttered curses and smiled at Tom. "Are you willing to help me do that very deed?" The smile on her face lit up her violet eyes with mischief, and Tom burst out laughing.

"How are we going to do it?" he replied.

The noise downstairs in the lodging house grew louder, shouts echoing up the stairwell as someone rushed in to speak to the landlady.

Having retrieved their baggage, with Tom carrying most of it, including what Josh had left behind, they descended the stairs. They found the landlady brimming with dramatic news.

"A rider has just come in from Nowhere. There's been another murder there. The gold miner was found beside his diggings this morning. Same as before, killed with the words 'GOLD FEVER' written on a piece of board beside him and a bag of pebbles on his chest. You'd best not go back there, it's too dangerous. Nowhere is a dangerous place."

With difficulty, they extricated themselves from her excited chatter. Another man entering received most of the news from her, and as they walked away down the street they could still hear her voice.

"Where will we find the man selling the property claims?" Tom asked.

"I wonder if he has a place of business or whether he just does it in the saloon?" Cassidy replied. "Let's take this luggage up to the hotel and then we can have a look around for him."

They walked on, Tom struggling with the bags, but he was still guarding Cassidy from clumsy pedestrians and those who, eyeing her, made as if to talk to her. In a town struck by gold fever, any woman was unusual. A beautiful woman was not only rare but a focal point for all eyes. They entered the hotel and went up to the rooms they had been given alongside the Duke of Ravenswood.

"To think we were traveling with the Duke of Ravenswood! I can't believe it," muttered Tom as he followed Cassidy up the stairs.

She paused, looked back at him, and chuckled. "I don't think he can believe it, either."

They walked into the room to find a heated exchange going on between Josh and the young tutor. A silence fell, making Cassidy and Tom feel uncomfortable.

Then Josh got up from his chair and walked over to the window. With his back to the room and to those seated within it, his voice came out in a harsh, angry manner. "He wants me to go back to England. Immediately. Take the boy back and live there. I can't remember the place; I don't want to remember it. My life is here, out West. I work in the general store, and I'm happy with my life. What do I know or remember of being a duke in an enormous house or castle or whatever?" He swung around and glared at the young man. "Do you know what you're asking of me? And this boy you say is my son—I don't know him. He doesn't know me."

Josh walked toward Cassidy, his voice changing, becoming almost pleading. "What should I do? He"— Josh gestured to the young man who sat in the chair, almost frozen in stunned silence—"wants me to go back to England at once. If I don't, he's going to go back himself and take the boy to some uncle. I am the heir to this vast estate, but the boy is next in line."

Cassidy sank down on the nearest chair and looked from one to the other. There was an expectant silence in the room, but she didn't know what to say. The seriousness of Josh's predicament hung heavily in the air, each of them waiting for some kind of resolution. And they were waiting for Cassidy to find the answer to Josh's problem. What could she say? How could she find the answer?

CHAPTER FIFTEEN

"Wait one moment, please," Cassidy said as she gracefully exited the room. She made her way into the kitchen and paused at the doorway, her gaze resting on the little boy, Charles. The kitchen, a large wooden structure attached to the main hotel building, was filled with a mingling of steam and rich cooking aromas. The potent scent of food was nearly overwhelming to Cassidy, who was now hungry.

Activity buzzed at one end of the kitchen, where three people tended to the pots and pans on a wood-fired stove. They moved back and forth with remarkable speed and coordination, never colliding with one another. At the other end, a table surrounded by chairs sat ready for the next meal, with cold dishes already set out. Seated at an empty table nearby was a small woman and the little boy, Charles. The child flicked back his blond hair, revealing a striking resemblance to Josh. He was engrossed in play and chatting happily with the woman. As he yawned, a look of tender affection crossed the woman's face, and she gently wrapped an arm around him. Cassidy had seen enough.

"The woman with Charlie? Who is she?" Cassidy asked Jones as she re-entered the room.

"That first day we arrived, she helped us settle the boy down. It's been difficult for him because Mr. Duke took him away without his nurse," Jones replied, looking down at his shoes with an enormous sigh. "The nurse took one look at the ship and the sea, fainted, and then went home."

"What shall I do, Cassidy?" Josh repeated his question, his voice tinged with desperation.

"The boy needs that woman he's with. He knows her and is happy with her. Will she travel with you, Jones?" Cassidy asked, not waiting for his response before continuing. "He needs to get to know you, Josh. You're his father. Whether it's on the journey back to England or staying here for a while, it doesn't matter. He needs a home, and he needs you."

The silence that followed was heavy until Josh broke it. "What's happening in England now, with the estate?"

Jones took a deep breath before answering. "The estate is being looked after by your uncle and cousin. They've lived there all their lives and know it well. Your uncle is an honest man and frequently clashed with your brother. He always suspected that you were taken prisoner by him and killed, but there was nothing he could do. Your uncle is a capable man and does everything with great care."

"Did I enjoy living in England? Was I happy managing the estate?" Josh asked, his intense gaze fixed on Jones. Cassidy sensed the importance of this answer and waited anxiously.

Jones fidgeted with his collar, taking a deep breath before he spoke. "To be honest, you were always restless. You did your duty, but you disliked the formality and rigidity of English life. You often expressed a desire to go to America, so much so that your brother must have found it amusing to send you off here."

"What would happen to the estate if I did not return?" Josh asked.

Jones stared at him, pausing to take another deep breath before replying. "You would deprive your son of his heritage, and the estate of its legal owner and master."

***

Next morning, as the horses were being readied beside the wagon, the group gathered. Cassidy walked up Main Street, accompanied by Tom and Josh. The lady from the kitchen, Ruth, who had been promoted to full-time nanny for Charles, and Charles himself—who now insisted everyone call him Charlie—joined them.

"You are doing the right thing, Josh. We'll all miss you. I'll explain everything to Manuel and Eliza at the general store. And"— here Cassidy patted the carpetbag she was carrying—"I have your letter for Amy in here."

As they approached the small group traveling to Nowhere by wagon, a tall Indian detached himself and, with his arm around the small woman at his side, brought her forward.

"Mother, this is Cassidy. She will be with you today in the wagon. Hello, Tom, are you ready to ride all the way to Nowhere?" This last remark was accompanied by a smile at the young Chinese boy, who was staring open-mouthed at the fine horses lined up at the hitching rail of the livery stables.

"Am I to ride one of those?"

"It's better than running beside it," teased Cassidy.

All laughed at this, but Cassidy noticed the fearful look and wide eyes of Miriam, Sam's mother, as she gazed at her. Cassidy's smart outfit and stylish hat were rare sights in Nowhere, but for the woman who grew up among Indians it was a sight to behold.

"Have you heard the latest news from Nowhere?" Sam said. "There's been another murder. This is the third one. This time, it was another gold prospector who was found outside the saloon."

"The same as before?" Josh asked.

"Yes, the words 'GOLD FEVER' and the bag of

pebbles, just the same as before."

"The wagon is ready. Climb aboard." A box was put down at the back of the wagon, and the two women were ushered in first. Three more people joined them. Cassidy was relieved there were no more. She had heard that sometimes wagons going to Nowhere and its newfound gold fields could be crammed. Under her long eyelashes, she scrutinized them, including a large, older man—a workman of some sort—carrying an oversized canvas bag. Full of tools, she thought. He must be a prospector, Cassidy thought, then transferred her gaze to the other two who were sitting together. The younger one had not stopped talking since he got onto the wagon, and it looked as if he would not stop anytime soon. What he was talking about, Cassidy couldn't quite hear. It could annoy her, but if she wanted to doze on the journey, it could be a blessing. In seconds, the wagon lumbered off, and the chorus of goodbyes from Josh, and especially Charlie, could be heard.

Sitting back with a sigh, she placed her carpetbag in the space beside her. Without staring at Miriam, all this while Cassidy had been watching her out of the corner of her eye. She saw the nervous fingers with the small piece of material on the edge of her scarf, twisting it between her fingers again and again. Sidelong glances from beneath Miriam's eyelashes darted across to the other occupants before they finally came to rest on Cassidy. Miriam was startled. She hadn't expected Cassidy to be looking at her.

"What a long, boring journey we have now," Cassidy said.

"Yes." The word was just a breathy answer.

Cassidy decided chatting to Miriam would be useless.

She didn't want to, anyway. She wanted to sit back, close her eyes, and think.

Josh, along with his young son, nanny Ruth, and the tutor Jones, would embark later today on the long trip back to England. It was the best thing for Josh to do. It was the only thing. She would be sorry to see him go. For a while, she had found him charming and had almost fancied herself falling in love with him. But she hadn't fallen for him. She could wave him off to England with no damage at all to her heart and wish him well on his journey. Josh was out of her mind now.

Cassidy now had to concentrate on the man who was selling to people the claims—false claims—upon her land. Cassidy sat on the hard seat being jostled and bounced around all the way to Nowhere. But all she was conscious of was how her mind went round and round in circles. There were two people she needed to capture or kill: the Pebble Killer, as he was now being called, and the fraudulent businessman who was swindling gold-fever-hungry prospectors. They were coming into Nowhere, and Cassidy opened her eyes. Perhaps her thoughts had ended up in a slight doze because here she was, arriving at the livery stables.

Miriam, opposite her, had also dozed. Fearful of being asked questions and having to make polite conversation with the beautiful blonde creature who had sat down opposite her, she had tried to stay awake. Miriam had been puzzled by Cassidy's silence. But it had made her relax in the other woman's company, which was what Cassidy wanted.

"Is Sam taking you to Dry Creek Ranch now?" Cassidy asked Miriam.

"Yes, he says Amy wants me to come back to live

with Sam and my nephew, David." The reply was given to Cassidy, a worried frown on Miriam's face.

"Amy will welcome you. I think she finds it hard work running the ranch and looking after the children. You will be a great help to her."

At Cassidy's words, Miriam looked at her, and for the first time, she gave a slight smile. "I can help Amy?"

"Yes, she will be glad to see you. Can you give her this letter? Tell her I should be along to see her in the next few days if I don't see her in Nowhere itself." The box was carefully placed for their descent from the wagon, and they were met by Tom and Sam.

"We have work to do, Tom," murmured Cassidy to the young Chinese boy as they were about to walk along Nowhere's Main Street to the hotel. "A killer and a fraudulent businessman. Which one will we find first?"

Tom's voice was a mere whisper, but it reached Cassidy's ears. She laughed out loud at the whispered remark, her violet eyes twinkling as she looked at the boy beside her and murmured under her breath. "Of course, we'll kill them!"

CHAPTER SIXTEEN

The wagon had been driven into the back of the livery stables where a large yard spread out, bustling with activity. Sam had come up to them after helping his mother to a small buggy. He gently assisted her into the buggy, then retraced his steps to Cassidy and Tom. "I'm taking my mother to Dry Creek Ranch. Are you going to ..." He paused, giving Cassidy a penetrating stare.

"Am I going to search out and stop these fraudulent mining claims?" Cassidy finished for him, a sweet smile crossing her lips as she gazed up at him.

Sam shook his head. "Cassidy, you look like the most perfect, beautiful woman I have ever seen. But I know you to be the deadliest killer I have ever met!"

Even Tom smiled at this remark, and both men looked to Cassidy to see her reaction. She threw her head back, her blonde curls dancing beneath the pretty green bonnet she was wearing. Her eyes sparkled with mischief, and her pearly teeth shone in her laughing smile.

"It's nice to know that your friends understand and respect you," Cassidy said, putting an arm through each of the men beside her. She whispered to both of them, "I'll make enquiries at the hotel where I'll stay. Both of you ask around for any information you can get about this crook. Also, find out about the Pebble Killer."

Sam and Tom agreed to this and exchanged a look. Sam shrugged. "Keep a lookout. This town has become dangerous. Tom, watch over her. I'll settle my mother at the ranch and then I think I might come back to Nowhere."

Cassidy stared at Sam. "Why are you going to come back? There's no need."

The usually emotionless face of the tall, handsome part Indian broke into a broad smile. "What? And miss all the fun? I know you, Cassidy. When you get going, there's always plenty of action. I wouldn't want to be left out of that!"

Sam walked off, leaving Cassidy smiling at his retreating back. Tom was much like Sam, someone who usually hid his emotions, but he couldn't stop himself from laughing out loud.

The buggy with Sam and his mother drove out of the livery stable yard. Tom and Cassidy, carrying their baggage with Tom, shouldering most of it, also left the yard. The noise outside was horrendous. People were everywhere, the majority of them men clad in dirty work clothes, mud-spattered and surly-faced. The town had become engulfed in gold fever.

"We'd best get to the hotel quickly," Tom said, hoisting the baggage over his shoulder and under one arm, leaving his other arm free to escort Cassidy up Main Street. The sidewalks of wooden planks were now muddy and treacherous underfoot. A recent rain shower had done little to stop the place from becoming a mud-soaked mess.

For once, Cassidy was comforted by the young man beside her. Tom, similar in height to Cassidy, was slimly built but with broad shoulders and an air of self-confidence in his fighting abilities. All went well until they neared the sheriff's office. A group of four men staggered out of the saloon, drunk and shouting as they staggered along the sidewalk. They saw Cassidy and, dismissing the young man beside her as inconsequential, blocked her way.

"Excuse me, I need to pass," Cassidy said in a cool,

clear voice.

The men laughed. One slapped another on the back and sneered at Cassidy. "Lady needs to pass," he mocked, making his companions laugh harder.

"Don't think we'll let you pass. You look like you need some fun. I reckon we can make sure you get it." The leader, a tall, thin man with mud-spattered trousers, a dirty flannel shirt and a grimy face with whiskers, took a step toward her. The smell of sweat and mining work made Cassidy step back.

That was a mistake. He took it as a sign of weakness and reached out an arm toward her.

That was his mistake!

A slim hand shot out, and in a moment he was on the ground howling in pain as Cassidy had his hand in an agonizing position. His friends couldn't believe their eyes. The tiny creature before them had the hard man of the group on his knees. He struggled so hard to get away from her, they could all hear his wrist snap.

"You're lucky. Others who tried to touch her ended up dead. Let him go, Cassidy. Get back to your diggings, and don't come into my town again!" Lance Grey, the sheriff, drawled from his office door. He stood there leaning against the doorjamb, a smile upon his face. He shook his head as the man with the broken wrist clambered to his feet and led the others back down the street toward the mountainside, where they were digging for gold.

"I reckon you're just back. First sign of trouble and you're in it, and you haven't even unpacked yet," Grey said, turning and walking back into the sheriff's office, firmly closing the door behind him.

Cassidy stared at the closed door, and then she and

Tom continued to the hotel. All the while, she wondered about this sheriff. She had no difficulty sizing up people, especially men. With her beauty, she had to be on alert for unwanted advances. Somehow, she couldn't understand what manner of man the sheriff was. He was the only man she'd ever met who understood her. Grey understood what drove her to kill evil men and end their killing sprees. He didn't condemn her. He didn't try to stop her. But Cassidy was furious that he laughed at her.

Dora welcomed them both back. Like the hotel in Duloe and the lodging house there, Dora's hotel was full to bursting. Tom shared a room with the two men who worked for Dora, while Cassidy had a small room beside Dora's. Cassidy didn't care where she slept. She was so tired after that horrible wagon journey. First, though, she had to go to the general store. She had to give the letter to Manuel that Josh had written for him, along with the gold nuggets Josh had intended for the general store owners.

Tom escorted her there, and this time they got there with no incidents from the throng of miners. Cassidy had borrowed a duster coat from Dora, as well as one of Dora's oldest bonnets, so passed unnoticed.

A few hours later, Cassidy returned to the hotel. She was met by Dora, who saw the exhaustion on her face and put an arm around her.

"It was difficult, wasn't it? They found it hard to believe that Josh was actually a duke and owned a stately home in England, I expect. I can't believe it either. Here, in the middle of Nowhere, we actually had a duke living with us! Cassidy, you look exhausted. Off you go up to your room. I'll bring you some food up in a little while."

Cassidy gave Dora a weak smile. "Thank you." Trudging up to her room, she opened the door with a sigh of relief. Alone at last. The first thing she did was turn to the jug of water and wash. The dust from the journey had been thick, and even walking down the street seemed to coat everything she was wearing.She sat on the bed, just staring out of the window onto the street below.

CHAPTER SEVENTEEN

"Cassidy, I have your meal for you. Eat this and have a good rest. After breakfast, perhaps you can have a chat with me about everything. I've an idea of how to get more information about the fraudulent crook selling the maps and false claims," Dora said as she placed the tray on the dressing table.

Cassidy ate the meal in front of her, barely remembering what she had eaten by the time she finished. Curling up on the bed, she soon slept.

It was late when she heard the noise. For a moment, she wondered where she was. Abruptly, she sat up in bed. The window showed a sliver of moonlight coming between the curtains she had drawn earlier that night. Tired though she was, she had drawn the curtains, locked her door, and placed her pistol under her pillow and her knife in its sheath on the nightstand beside her. She reached over from the bed and pulled back one curtain. It was enough for the moonlight to light up the door. The noise continued as someone tried to pick the lock.

"Not very good at it, are you?" she muttered to herself. By this time, she was on the far side of the bed, crouched down behind it, with only her head and her hand holding the pistol above the bed itself.

Finally, the lock clicked open. She watched the doorknob slowly turn. The door creaked open, slowly revealing a figure creeping inside with a knife in hand. The moonlight caught the blade, sparking a flash of light. It showed the man from the street. He stepped forward, toward the bed.

Cassidy, despite her haste, had stuffed one pillow underneath the covers, making it look as if she was still sleeping.

"Make a fool of me, bitch? I don't think so. But I'm not taking any chances this time. You can die for what you did to my wrist. Take that, bitch!" The knife was raised and plunged down with all the man's force behind it. He gasped in surprise as the knife went into the pillow.

"It's me who's not taking any chances. You are going to die this time, not me," Cassidy said, standing up and facing the man.

He jumped back from the bed, his face a mask of horror, his mouth agape at the sight of the gun held by the pretty woman across the bed. He could see in her eyes that there was no mercy for him. There was no way she would let him live now, after he had attempted to kill her.

Hurriedly, he stepped back—but it was no good. The bullet struck his forehead, and he fell backward onto the carpet. The noise of the gunfire brought Dora rushing into the room. She stood on the threshold, a scream dying in her throat as she looked down at the man.

"I made sure he died falling onto the rug on the floor. I didn't want you to have to wash bloodstained linen," Cassidy said calmly. The doorway filled with people eagerly peering in at the sight of the dead man.

Dora turned toward the older of her two menservants. "Take him out the back and to the sheriff's office."

Tom, who had rushed up the stairs, now stood looking down at the man. "He's the one who attacked you on Main Street, isn't he?" Tom asked.

"Yes, somehow he picked the lock, came in with a knife and stabbed my pillow. It was meant to be me who died by his knife." Cassidy said. "Please, can everyone go away? I'm so tired. I just want to get back to sleep."

"The lock on that door is broken. You can't sleep in here," Dora said.

"I'm not moving my stuff now, not at this hour of the night. The blood is gone; the body is gone. I'll put something against the door. I need my sleep," Cassidy insisted.

The body had been removed. The maid had taken away the bloodstained rug, and now the room looked as if nothing had happened.

Dora stared at Cassidy, twisting her hands, unsure of what to do. The calm manner of Cassidy made her gasp.

"Don't worry, Dora," Tom said as they both watched Cassidy climb back into bed. "I'll sleep here behind the door. I'll put the chair there and stay here all night."

CHAPTER EIGHTEEN

Cassidy was jolted awake by the sudden shouting outside. The commotion was followed by a scream and then more shouts.

"What is it? What's happening outside?" Cassidy asked, slipping out from under the covers. She stood at the window, pushing the curtain aside just enough to see without being seen.

Tom, who had been sleeping in the chair behind the door, followed her to the window.

"It's the Pebble Killer again. He's killed this young man," a shrill voice outside revealed the cause of the disturbance. Cassidy pulled the curtain back further to get a better view.

Below her, on the street opposite, she saw the crumpled figure of a young man. A full bag of pebbles sat on his chest, and the remnants of his life lay scattered around him: a pickaxe, a metal pan, and a small empty canvas bag—evidence of his fruitless search for gold.

The crowd quieted and parted for the tall figure of Sheriff Lance Grey. Tall and thin, his black-clad figure beneath the window seemed menacing enough without him looming over the dead body. He turned to the smaller man who had followed him, and Cassidy realized this must be the new deputy. At a gesture from Grey, the deputy collected the young man's belongings, and Lance knelt beside the body, taking the bag of pebbles and a note. He signalled to the burly man from the livery stables, who had taken it upon himself to bury people in the freshly dug cemetery up on the hill. The two lawmen turned and walked back toward the sheriff's office. Before he did so, Grey glanced upward, as if conscious of

Cassidy's gaze upon him. Their eyes met for a brief moment, and then he was gone.

Tom went downstairs to get breakfast for himself and Cassidy, so giving her time to change for the day ahead. She proposed breakfasting in her room before beginning the search for the man selling the false claims. When Dora came in with her breakfast, Dora told Cassidy about the man and how he wandered up and down Nowhere on Main Street in the morning, seeking likely victims.

Dora thought Cassidy might find him sitting in the new cafe that had sprung up near the saloon. "It's a meeting place for people. Just like the saloon, but without the booze. Respectable people have coffee there or even a light meal, like breakfast or lunch. There are two cafes, but the one further up the hill caters more to the working men. Our fraudulent businessman wouldn't get much money out of people there. He tends to look for easy pickings in the saloon or at this cafe."

"I remember Charles Roberts, who was also selling land. Admittedly, they did get some land, but it was poor quality, unable to farm or grow anything on it. But he had an office."

Dora placed the tray with breakfast on the dressing table. "Nothing like that with this man," she said as she walked toward the door. "He doesn't plan on staying long. I think he will take as much money as he can and then disappear before everybody realizes what he's doing."

Leaving the hotel, Cassidy and Tom paused for a moment to look at where the man had been murdered, both taking in the details with a single glance before moving on. They didn't want to draw attention to themselves. Despite Cassidy dressing in a drab green dress and jacket with one of her trademark hats, she still stood out among the motley crowd on Nowhere Main Street.

Cassidy had enjoyed the breakfast Dora had brought up for her. She wasn't hungry, but she went into the cafe with a sign outside that just said "Eats". Tom had eaten his breakfast downstairs with the men, but showed all the signs of imminent starvation despite, having had a huge plateful. Assured by him that he would eat anything and everything she ordered, they went and sat at a window seat in the Eats cafe. A glance around the steamy room showed Cassidy that it was a mixed crowd. Some were miners, with the tools of their trade at their feet. Two or three of them sat together, talking endlessly and quietly, as if discussing a secret claim. Cassidy wondered if they'd already struck it rich and were now wondering what to do. On the far wall against the back, under a flapping, tent-like awning, sat three ladies. Respectable, thought Cassidy. They eyed her the moment she stepped inside.

She was glad to have Tom beside her. He looked insignificant, but she was aware of his powerful martial arts knowledge and his improving skills in the knife techniques she was teaching him. His ability to draw a gun and shoot had been honed on Broken Horseshoe Ranch by Luke and his daughter Amy. With a slim build and slicked-back hair, he could easily be passed over as a nondescript, ineffectual young Chinese boy. Cassidy was pleased to have him go unobserved because she knew about his talents. Everyone assumed he was her manservant, a pretence Cassidy did not like to maintain, but Tom accepted, and even enjoyed going unnoticed. So they sat, waiting for their second breakfast. Their cups of coffee had been refilled twice as they watched the man at the far end of the room, with the wood-fired stoves producing breakfast after breakfast for the constant stream of people coming in and out.

"It's large," Cassidy murmured, looking down at the plate in front of her. Swimming in grease were the bacon, eggs and biscuits, with a weak, watery gravy over all of it. She couldn't help it. Her nose wrinkled in disgust, and she whispered out of the side of her mouth, "I can't eat any of this. Can you?"

Tom's whispered reply came back, "No, I don't think I can, not after my meal at Dora's."

A young man and his very pregnant wife sat at the table beside them. Cassidy had noticed that under the table he was counting out their money. There didn't seem to be much of it. Leaning over slightly, Cassidy murmured, "My companion ordered this by mistake. It's untouched. Could you eat it for me? It seems a shame to waste it."

The hand holding the coins closed tightly over them, and they both stared at the plate of food with eager eyes. Then the woman looked at Cassidy. "If you really don't want it ..." Tom jumped to his feet and carefully took their plates over to the next table. Then he went back and took the plate of biscuits, which again had been uneaten by both of them, and placed it on their table.

"Thank you, but ..." The young woman, her white face drawn and tired, looked at the plate and then at Cassidy. "Thank you."

"Eat it while it's hot," Cassidy said and turned away to give the young couple peace to eat and divide the meals between them.

"I don't see anyone with maps or papers," Cassidy

said quietly to Tom.

"No, perhaps he's not here yet. Shall I get more coffee so we can stay longer?" Tom replied.

Both of them had only taken one sip of the dreadful coffee. Cassidy whispered to Tom, "This isn't made from coffee beans, is it?"

"No, I don't think the coffeepot has ever seen a coffee bean," was Tom's reply. Cassidy gave a snort of laughter. Tom spoke very little, but sometimes he came out with the sharpest, wittiest remarks.

Nevertheless, giving her a rueful glance, he rose and got more coffee for them. He stood with the coffee cups, looking down at Cassidy and inclining his head toward the table beside them. Catching his meaning, Cassidy said, "Good idea."

The coffee cups were placed in front of the young couple, who had devoured the food given to them by Cassidy. She leaned over toward them. "We are waiting for someone, and I thought we'd better order more coffee. Please do drink it. I can't drink any more."

"Thank you. We are also waiting for someone," the young man said. "He has maps and can sell claims for land that is sure to hold gold. We met with him yesterday and some other people who are keen to buy these claims. It was amazing!" His voice rose in excitement as he told Cassidy and Tom.

His wife also beamed at them. "He just banged a rock with a hammer, and you could see gold flakes inside. Seemingly, underneath these rocks there are gold nuggets. Somehow, we managed to get enough money together to buy a claim."

Tom groaned audibly. Cassidy kicked him under the table. Now she didn't know what to say or do. If she told the couple they were wasting their money and the man was a fraud, there would be a lot of questions and cries of alarm and disbelief. The whole place would be in an uproar within minutes. Cassidy felt strange, unsure of what to say or do. It was Tom who saved the situation. He also leaned toward the young couple from their table. "That sounds like a marvellous idea. Do you think he would have any spare claims for myself and my mistress to buy? I have a younger brother, and I'm certain he would like to join me in digging for gold."

The two young people gazed at them both and beamed. "I'm certain he has more of them. It would be so good if you had a claim next to ours," said the young woman, smiling shyly at Cassidy.

Before she could stop herself, Cassidy said, "How lovely. We could have tea with each other in the afternoons."

It was with absolute horror that Cassidy realized the young woman, obviously pregnant, smiled back as if that could be a possibility. Cassidy saw Tom's mouth drop open as he too understood the absolute ignorance of this couple about the life they would lead on a gold field.

"Here he comes!" The young man stood up and waved. It was answered by a wave from the man who had just entered.

Overweight, with oily black hair slicked down, and wearing a suit made of a checked material suitable only for a city, not a frontier town, the man carried a leather briefcase under his arm and had a smile that was more of a sneer, Cassidy thought. But his dark brows hid eyes that roamed the cafe, looking for prospective customers, and those eyes were as hard as granite.

Tom muttered something under his breath. Cassidy

turned to him, "What's that, Tom?"

"An evil man. He has a false smile."

"Let's hope you and I, Tom, can wipe that smile on his fat face."

CHAPTER NINETEEN

Cassidy took the map and claim form from Oliver, as she had been instructed to call him. When he sat down at the table beside the young couple, Cassidy noticed his calculating eyes appraising the cost of her outfit, from her shoes to her bonnet. Once he finished his mental tally, he scanned the room for other potential customers for his gold claims.

She glanced at the claim form, recognizing it as a worthless piece of paper filled with just enough legal jargon to confuse prospective gold miners. But it was the map that caught her attention. It detailed every aspect of her actual property, from the creek that wound down the mountain to the rocks and canyons and extending into the foothills and peaks. Where had he got this detailed map from?

"This is a very detailed map, Oliver," Cassidy said. "It's quite hard to understand." As expected, this comment coaxed him into the role of a knowledgeable, kindly uncle. He began explaining the map, and she nodded knowingly, feigning approval of his expertise.

"Where did you get a map with such detail?" she asked. Upon noticing Tom's sudden interest in her question, she observed him taking a map from the young man, who had placed it on the table while signing the claim form. She felt Tom stiffen beside her, realizing he recognized it as an actual drawing of her property.

"I bought this from a friend who has sold me a few other properties around Nowhere. Wonderful place." Oliver said.

Cassidy hoped Tom wouldn't give away her next ruse and was thankful for his inscrutable expression when she said. "My father was hoping to buy a ranch around here. Have you heard of any for sale?"

Cassidy almost saw the dollar signs flash in Oliver's hard eyes as he reached for the briefcase beside his chair. With a flourish, he produced three documents and handed them to her. "I wonder if your father would be interested in any of these ranches that are up for sale? Will he be joining you shortly? I'd love to show them to him—and you, of course." He spread the documents out on the table, pushing the half-full coffee cups to one side, heedless of the splashes.

"Oh, what unusual names they have! This one is called Dry Creek Ranch. Is it always dry? Would that be a problem?" Cassidy's artless questions made Oliver smile. He leaned over and patted her hand, and it took all of Cassidy's willpower not to pull hers away from his greasy fingers.

"My dear, it's only dry in summer. But it's no problem. Look here, this Granger Ranch is adjacent, and there's an agreement that water from their river is always available."

"Is that for sale, too?"

"Yes, sad to say the owners have decided to retire. They've grown old and find the life difficult. So, you see, there are three for sale, all at wonderful prices. The other one on the market is called Broken Horseshoe Ranch. Do you think your father would be interested in any of them?"

"I'm sure he would. In fact, I think I will go telegraph him immediately about these wonderful opportunities you have." Cassidy stood up, smiling at the young couple and Oliver, and left the cafe.

"They're not for sale!" Tom exclaimed angrily as

Cassidy marched up Main Street. "That's fraud."

Cassidy, too angry to respond, shoved the sheriff's office door open with such force it banged against the wall. Sheriff Lance Grey looked up from his coffee.

"Can't you just open the door normally? What is it now?"

"These are for sale in the cafe, by a man called Oliver, along with false claims he's selling to would-be gold miners. Look." From beneath her jacket, she pulled out the maps of the properties she had taken from Oliver. "This is fraud."

Tom laughed, and both Cassidy and the sheriff stared at him in amazement. "That man, 'call me Oliver', tried to sell Cassidy her own ranch and her property on Devil's Mountain. He was selling them to the actual owner!"

"Where is his body? Did you knife him or shoot him?" Grey asked Cassidy.

"He's still alive in the cafe. I walked out before I did anything," Cassidy admitted.

"I'm amazed at your self-control, Cassidy," said Grey with a sly smile at her. Grey reached for his coat, shrugged it on, adjusted his gun holster, and pulled another gun from a drawer, sliding it into his boot.

"I suppose you want to come with me, Cassidy?" he drawled.

Shaking her head, Cassidy walked out the door. "No, thanks. I don't want anyone to know what I own in this area. Not yet. Go and arrest that crook and try to return some of the money to the poor gold miners he's swindled.

"Come along, Tom, we need to hurry," Cassidy said.

CHAPTER TWENTY

"Come on, Tom," Cassidy urged, grabbing his arm and pulling him toward the livery stable. "Hurry up. Let's get there before Grey thinks to see what's been going on there."

Pushing their way through the bustling crowd, Cassidy moved almost unnoticed in the garments she had borrowed, again from Dora: a drab duster coat and large bonnet. Tom had to dash to keep up with her fast pace.

"Why? What's at the livery stables?" Tom panted as they reached the stable yard.

"Didn't you notice that the young man who was killed was dry?" Cassidy asked, pausing to scan the stable yard for anyone.

Shaking his head, Tom replied, "What difference does that make, Cassidy?"

"It means he was sheltering from the early rain shower. Where would a hard-up young mining prospector shelter cheaply?" She pointed to the far end of the stables, where some stalls had been divided into sleeping spaces. Cassidy knew Josh had spent many nights there, and those arriving late at night were grateful for the cheap shelter.

"How will we know which one he slept in?" Tom asked, fully on board with Cassidy's idea and eager to help. Before they could do anything, the old man Curly, who rented out the stable cots, walked toward them.

"You ask him, Tom. Curly hates women," Cassidy hissed under her breath as he approached.

"What should I say?" Tom hissed back, wondering how to inquire about the dead man's sleeping spot.

"I don't know. Think of something yourself, Tom!"

Cassidy snapped as Curly neared.

"My friend," Tom stammered, "he stayed with you last night, just came off the wagon from Duloe—reckons he left a boot behind. I said I'd look for it. Young chap, could you tell me which stall he slept in?"

To his astonishment, Curly responded with a loud honking cough, casting a suspicious glance at Cassidy, who snuggled deeper into her coat. "Easy enough. Only one who stayed last night. Far stall. Haven't tidied up yet, just rake them over each day. Been busy with the horses. Go look for yourselves." He stomped away, coughing again. "Paid for two nights he did, thinking he's gonna become rich and find lots of gold. Another stupid fool."

Cassidy lifted her long skirts and ran toward the stall Curly had pointed out. On their knees, she and Tom rummaged through the straw, hoping to find something. At the back, pushed under a large pile of straw, they found a small notebook and one of the maps Oliver had been selling. The claim form beside it told them everything they needed to know. Now they understood why the young man had come to Nowhere. But who had killed him? And why?

Rising to her feet, Cassidy brushed the straw from her skirt and looked around. There were no other hiding places. Coming to the livery stable had been a good idea. She slipped the journal, map, and form into her bag, and looked at Tom. "That's done, Tom. Let's get out of here before Grey finds us."

As they walked away, Tom asked, "What about the stuff we found? Will you give it to Grey?"

Surprised, Cassidy stopped and looked at him, ignoring the muttered curses of a man who narrowly missed falling over her. "Of course, Tom. This might help him in his search for the Pebble Killer. But only after I finish reading it and finding out whatever there is to help us in our search."

Still worried, Tom pressed: "If you give it to Grey, won't he be mad at you for keeping it?"

"I won't give it to him myself, Tom. Perhaps it will be found and handed in to him. Or it can be posted through that empty window with no bars. Yes, that would solve the problem!" Cassidy laughed.

Tom didn't share her amusement. He was certain Grey would realize Cassidy had the information first. But without proof, what could he do?

Back in her room, Cassidy examined the map for additional marks, but found none. At first sight, the claim form, with its fancy lettering, gave the impression of being genuine. This scam had been well executed. On the form was described a small parcel of land and bore the name of the dead boy.

The journal, written in a childish hand, started the day he left his family farm. Against his family's wishes, he set out to become rich and help them with his gold. He detailed his arrival in Duloe, planning to go to the other gold fields. But he met Oliver and, falling for his charm, gave him his last coins for the map and claim. Then he described his journey to Nowhere.

"He wrote this last night. There's no mention of anyone likely to be a killer. He must have met the man who killed him after leaving the livery stable," Cassidy pointed to the page describing the stable. Then there was nothing.

"I was so sure there must be some clue in here." In frustration, she flung the journal onto the table. It flew off the edge and hit the floor, splitting open. A piece of paper peeked out from the binding.

Tom pounced on it and pulled it from the journal.

"This must be something he meant to keep hidden. It's all creased. I'll smooth it out on the table."

Both stood side by side, peering down as Tom smoothed the paper.

"What does it say?" Tom asked.

CHAPTER TWENTY-ONE

The writing and markings on the map were faint, making it difficult to decipher at first. Cassidy's finger traced a line that spanned almost the entire paper. "I think this is the creek running down from the high peak of Devil's Mountain. Surely, that's where they're digging for gold right now?"

"That cross has to mean something important," Tom said, puzzled. He moved around the table to look at the paper from a different angle.

"I think those squiggles represent the clifftop dwellings. It's on the opposite side of the ridge from Broken Horseshoe Ranch. I've never been that way, have you, Cassidy?"

Slowly, Cassidy shook her head. "No, I've never been that way." She followed the line again, staring intently at the map. "Do you think this could be a hideout? If so, why did he hide it in the binding of his journal? It was meant to be kept secret. Who gave it to him? Was he planning to go up there?" Her finger hovered over the cross.

It was Tom who found the real clue. He had picked the journal up from the floor, where it had fallen and broken apart, revealing a piece of paper. Now, he lifted the journal from the table and began feeling around the covers. The cover that had held the paper was empty. Then Tom turned to the other cover. At first, he found nothing; it was still intact. Feeling it carefully, he noticed that the stitching at the top did not match the rest of the stitching around the book's cover. He reached for the knife Cassidy had left on the nightstand after breakfast. Inserting it between the mismatched stitches, Tom carefully moved the knife along the newer stitching. The thread came out easily, and he continued pulling it out.

Cassidy watched Tom closely, her interest evident in the way she hovered over his careful hands. Breathless with anticipation, Tom put the knife down and delicately peeled back the inner cover.

A slip of paper fell onto the table. Made of the same paper as the larger map, it showed part of the creek and a small X marking a place labeled "the hut".

"What does this mean? What hut? Do you know this area?" Tom asked Cassidy. She placed both pieces of paper side by side and said quietly, "This is a real puzzle. You have the larger map showing the general area and this smaller map highlighting specific details. But you'd need to know the terrain yourself to find it."

"What are we going to do? Should we go up there ourselves and look for it?" Tom said. Cassidy took the large road map and walked over to the window, holding it up to study it in the full light of day.

"There's only one thing we can do. We take it to Grey and tell him what we found."

Cassidy was dressed that morning in a powder blue costume, with a matching hat adorned with a little frill and her trademark buttons down the front and at the cuffs. She had a pretty reticule that matched the suit perfectly, but she popped it into her carpetbag. The patterned carpetbag had wine-red and gold colors in a swirling decorative pattern. It wasn't too large for her to carry, but it certainly held a fair amount of objects. Tom was curious about what she had inside it. Knowing Cassidy as he did, he reckoned there might be quite a few weapons within it. Aware that her outfit would stand out among the drab workers and miners in the town who now thronged the sidewalks, Cassidy again donned a duster coat over her outfit. The hood covered her bonnet, and, with this on, she and Tom made their way to the sheriff's office.

"He's going to be mad. We shouldn't have messed around with the dead guy's stuff." Tom was wary of the sheriff; he found him disconcerting—not exactly afraid of him, but conscious of his unpredictable manner. However, like Cassidy and most of the townspeople of Nowhere, he trusted him and knew Sheriff Lance Grey to be an honorable man.

"I'll open the door, Cassidy," Tom said, scurrying in front of her. He remembered how the sheriff had been furious at Cassidy for slamming the door last time and denting his office wall.

Also remembering this, Cassidy smiled—but let Tom go first to open the door slowly and carefully.

As expected, Sheriff Lance Grey was standing beside his stove with his tin mug of coffee in his hand. "Coffee?" He gestured to the pot as they walked in.

"No, thanks," came their quick reply as he reached for the coffeepot. Neither of them felt strong enough to face the sheriff's preferred brew.

Cassidy placed her carpetbag on his desk, opened it, and produced the journal.

The coffeepot was carefully placed down on his desk, and he moved some papers aside and took the journal she held out to him.

"You were busy with the body, and I suddenly thought that he would …" began Cassidy.

"You also saw that he was dry and reckoned he must've been somewhere out of the rain. Curly told me you'd been looking at where he slept. Was this all you found when you searched the straw, Cassidy?" the sheriff said and smiled as he stooped and picked a stray piece of straw still clinging to her skirt.

Tom shuffled his feet nervously. He felt most uncomfortable. Was Cassidy's impetuous action going to get them both into trouble?

"Thanks, I'm glad you got there first. I reckon if you hadn't, somebody else would have, just to see what he'd left behind. They could well have beaten me to it. Was that all you found?"

Cassidy nodded. "It was hidden right in the back. Whether he left it there on purpose or forgot it, I couldn't tell."

"I read the journal, the last few pages, but there was nothing there. When I placed it back on the table, I dropped it, and the binding split open. We found these two pieces of paper."

Cassidy took out the two pieces of paper she'd folded inside the journal. She cast a playful at Tom, her eyes sparkling with mischief. She had thrown the journal in anger at its lack of clues, but she wasn't going to tell Grey that, and she hoped Tom wouldn't either.

Spreading out the creases, the sheriff looked at it and said, "I know where this is. An old man set up camp beside a dry riverbed. He was positive there was gold buried deep down at a bend in the old river. He reckoned there had been a waterfall and a plunge pool with gold lying at the bottom. With the water long gone, all he had to do was dig it up."

Tom's eyes sparkled with interest. "Did he find it? Did he find the gold?"

"Not to my knowledge. Could have, though. One day he was there; the next day he was gone. Maybe he found the gold and went off to enjoy it." The sheriff laughed, and the other two smiled.

"You want to go up there, Cassidy, and look for this Pebble Killer?" The sheriff's abrupt question made her jump. "Don't you? I expect you want to go even more now you know there's a bounty on his head. The townspeople and the bank in Duloe have put together a bounty for him. You like collecting bounties, don't you?"

The image of the young man lying dead, killed only a few short hours earlier, came into her head, and Cassidy shuddered at the cruelty and indignity enacted upon him. "I enjoy getting bounties, but I'd go after this man without a bounty. What he did was senseless and cruel. He has to be stopped."

The sheriff walked over to a hook on the wall, took down his coat and grabbed a few more things, including a spare gun, which he slipped into his boot. Folding the map, he gave it back to Cassidy. "I've no need of it."

He glanced up and down at Cassidy to check her readiness to ride and asked, "You two coming with me? If so, let's go!"

CHAPTER TWENTY-TWO

Ten minutes later, Tom led the way into the livery stable. His eager steps and excited expression betrayed his age. Still in his teens, the young Chinese boy seemed mature for his age in many ways, but sometimes his youth did appear—and this was one of those times. Cassidy, following him, saw Sheriff Lance Grey talking to another man. They were sorting out horses, and Grey led out one horse while the man followed him with another. Two stood ready at the hitching rail.

"Sam! What are you doing here? Are you coming with us?" Cassidy's smile was broad as she looked at the man. "Are you alone? Is Amy with you?" Sam gave a shy smile at the mention of Amy. They had been part of a group that rescued the family of Apache from the village clifftop dwellings high in the mountains. During that rescue, they barely escaped with their lives to Broken Horseshoe Ranch.

"No, I left her at Dry Creek Ranch. She's helping my mother settle in there. Though I reckon if she heard what you lot were up to, she'd want to come along."

No doubt she would, Cassidy thought. Cassidy's beauty made other women avoid her, fearing she might be conceited and unpleasant in her treatment of them. Far from the truth, Cassidy did not trade on her beauty and was always eager to befriend other women of her own age. Amy was a kindred spirit. Both of them relished the outdoor life, knew how to shoot and stand up for themselves, and both were, in some ways, lonely.

"Sheriff Grey, do we need anything else with us?" Tom asked the tall man who was soothing the large, rangy horse he was going to ride.

The sunlight shone on the glossy black coat of the horse and the shoulder-length black hair of the man talking to him. The warmth of the sun had finally made Sheriff Lance Grey remove the long black coat he was always usually seen in. Reaching up to his horse, Cassidy noted his powerful muscles and the way he gentled the horse with a firm command.

Without turning around, he called out to them. "Don't Sheriff Lance Grey me the whole time. I hate the name Lance, and I don't like being called sheriff all the time. Call me Grey—that's what I've always been known as."

The horse was now calm. He turned round and gave the two newcomers a quick glance and approving nod. Both were ready to ride, and both Tom and Cassidy carried only the essentials needed for the journey. "Let's go, then."

They rode off out of Nowhere, leaving the bustling town behind them. The noise faded away to the silence of the empty desert lands. For some time, they rode on, each lost in thought. The journey ahead could be fruitless. The map found in the journal was possibly a waste of time. But Grey, as they now called him, had told them of his finding a broken-down hut with an old man living in it some years ago. That would prove an ideal hiding place for someone who didn't want to be found and who plotted murder.

It was getting hot. They had been riding for some considerable time, and up ahead there was a ridge of rock leading up to the first of the canyons of Devil's Mountain. "Over there, time to get out of the sun. We all need a rest." They settled the horses, and then each one of them sat in the shade. Taking a sip of water from her canteen, Cassidy knew enough neither to gulp it nor drink too much of it. She firmly closed the lid on it and retreated to the cool shade beneath the sheltering rock. Cassidy was tired. Last night had been eventful, and she was now feeling fatigue creep over her.

"There's a spot further up the canyon, where there's usually a spring. Let's make for it and hope to bed down for the night," Grey said to them. Cassidy shaded her eyes to see the far distance. The peaks of Devil's Mountain were not easily spotted individually. In the distance, where she was looking, she'd hoped to see the clifftop village, and, further on in the flatlands of the desert, Broken Horseshoe Ranch. Nothing. Resigned to be away from the land that she knew, that traveled on before, she slumped back, taking advantage of the shade and the silence.

"Time to go," whispered Tom. Startled, Cassidy grabbed her gun before she realized where she was and who was speaking to her. She had dozed off.

Grey was right: it was the ideal spot to camp for the night. The water was fresh and even cold. "Spring comes straight from the earth, deep below," Grey said as they filled their canteens and he filled the coffeepot.

Smiles were exchanged between them as he fished around in his saddlebag for his coffee. If possible, he always bought pure coffee. They all asked for their coffee while it was still weak. None of them could face the stewed brew he loved.

"Don't think we need to keep watch, but we'll sleep with our backs against the cliff face. And keep the horses close by," Grey said.

Cassidy was sure that she wouldn't sleep, almost ashamed of having fallen asleep at their noonday rest stop. But to her surprise, she drifted off almost immediately. She woke to the fresh morning air of the mountains. The dawn light was creeping over Devil's Mountain, the sky a glorious sight. She pushed herself up with her back against the rock face to watch the sunrise. Cuddling into her blanket, she was aware of eyes upon her.

"Glorious, isn't it?" The soft whisper from Grey surprised her. He, too, was watching the sunrise, and somehow, in that early dawn light fresh from sleep, the cynical, hard face that Grey normally presented to the world was gone. It was more open and friendly. Then, like a shutter, the usual expression she knew returned. It didn't take long to eat quickly, saddle up, and ride out.

After about an hour, Grey stopped and looked around him. "There's been a landslide here. Must've been in the grim winter weather. Do you still have that map, Cassidy? I must make certain I'm on the correct ridgeline."

Passing him the map, Cassidy looked about her. The land was now rising slowly into the mountains. Cacti grew everywhere, rocks were dotted about with scrubby, spiky bushes beside them, and the sandy soil was interspersed with rocky outcrops. Looking back, the desert lands stretching toward Broken Horseshoe Ranch were flat in comparison, and the heat haze was shimmering already, despite it being only mid-morning.

"The air is cooler here. The higher up we go, the sun doesn't seem as strong, but it can still burn, Cassidy. Don't take your hat off," Sam warned her.

Grey pocketed the map and pointed around the rocky outcrop they were approaching. "This way, once we get past the landslide, I'm sure I'll remember the way."

Exhausted, they had gone on as long as they thought

the horses could cope with. They dismounted at the top of the ridgeline. One side was a sheer drop to a valley floor below, but on the other they could see a valley with a small creek running through it. Part of the valley had a steep slope leading up to a peak of Devil's Mountain, whereas the other was more level beside the creek.

"It's not dried up. The last time I came here, it was dry at this time of year, but there have been many storms over the last few days," said Grey, looking down at it.

"It was a hard winter, Grey. The snow was heavy and clung to the cliff and mountaintops until later in the spring. When it finally melted, there was far more snowmelt this year, which is why all the creeks and rivers are full flowing," Sam said.

Cassidy noticed him continually looking behind them and looked back herself, wondering if they were being followed.

Sam saw her looking and pointed. "Storm clouds coming this way. They look very black and threatening to me. There will be plenty of rain in those."

All Cassidy could think of was Dora's insistence on putting a rolled-up slicker in with her bedroll. It might well have been a stroke of luck, giving her cause to thank Dora. They rode on a bit more after the horses had rested, and Grey pointed to the small, dilapidated cabin clinging to the mountainside. Before it, the creek flowed, and behind it and to the side there was ample grazing and green grass.

"There's no horse there, and no smoke coming out," Sam said and rode forward a bit. Then he looked across to Grey and asked him, "Do we go straight down, or should we hide the horses up here and sneak down?"

Grey had dismounted, and they all followed suit.

"Over there, that group of trees makes an ideal spot to hide the horses. How about you and I go down some way, Sam? Cassidy and Tom stay here, watch the horses, and be on the lookout for anyone approaching."

Cassidy and Tom looked at each other. Both would have liked to have gone down to investigate the cabin, but they realized that Sam and Grey were the most skilled at stealth and could react swiftly if necessary. They just didn't have the same experience.

Sam went first. The Apache in him and the training he had received growing up in the Apache village were not wasted, Cassidy thought. As she watched him stealthily creep down to the back of the cabin, he was like a shadow. She had to admit, Grey was almost as good as Sam in his furtive movements.

"Look, Sam has reached the cabin. He's looking in the window," Tom hissed to her.

Sam and Grey came out of the cabin after a short while and ran back up to where Tom and Cassidy stood in the small stand of trees.

"It's him," Grey said. "We found pieces of parchment, even small pieces of wood with "GOLD FEVER" written on them. A great bucketful of small pebbles stood by the door."

"It looks like he keeps things from each of his victims. There's a shelf with odd photos, pieces of clothing, and watches, all taken from those he's killed," Sam said.

"Did you find out how he chose his victims?" Cassidy asked.

Both men were busy drinking from their canteens. Grey was the one who answered her. "Yes, there was a map with names written and crosses marking spots and a claim form beside each one."

Tom was puzzled by this and couldn't understand what Grey meant.

"Don't you think, Sam, from looking at that stuff in that cabin, this is the guy who salts the rocks for Oliver to come and crack them open to find the gold?" Grey asked.

Sam stood looking down at the cabin, thinking over all the deeds seen inside it, and nodded in agreement. "Yes, he's probably doing that now. Oliver must give him the names of future claim owners, and the crosses must mark the sites where he has to drill the holes and put in the gold."

Cassidy, who had been sitting on the fallen tree trunk, said, "That makes sense. That man Oliver would never dirty his hands to do their dirty work of salting the rocks. He must give our killer gold, though, to put in the rocks."

"There was no gold in there, but what I saw was fool's gold," Sam said.

Tom looked puzzled and asked, "What's fool's gold?"

"Pyrite—it's a form of rock that looks just like gold. Perhaps our man Oliver doesn't trust this guy enough to give him actual gold. And these new prospectors probably wouldn't know any different. If it's shiny gold-looking rocks, they must think they are nuggets."

They settled down to wait for the return of the Pebble Killer. Now they had found his lair, and they were determined to find him and take him back for justice to be done. They would wait, no matter how long it took.

CHAPTER TWENTY-THREE

It was late afternoon. Shadows of purple, blue and black gathered on the far side of the canyon wall. Where the setting sun fell in long streaks, the rock glowed brightly, creating a vivid contrast against the darkening backdrop.

Cassidy felt a gathering chill in the air and pulled her jacket tightly around herself. She shifted her muscles slightly, trying not to make a noise. They never knew when the man would arrive. She was stiff, and she knew that when he came they would have to act fast. She couldn't afford to be found with cramped or stiff muscles that wouldn't immediately work. It had been silent between them for some time, and she wondered what the others were thinking.

Then she heard it. Glancing at the others, she saw each one of them become alert in different ways. Tom moved slightly, his eyes growing wider; Sam stiffened, though she couldn't imagine how she knew that because his body had been immobile in the same position since he took cover; Grey showed the most motion: like Tom, his eyes widened, his nostrils flared and his hands clenched tightly.

A rider on horseback rode up to the cabin, followed by a mule laden with baggage. "Looks like he's been resupplying," whispered Grey to the others under the cover of hoofbeats. Hitching his horse to the rail, the man moved inside the cabin. He began unloading the mule, and that's when Grey gave the signal.

Inch by inch, they crept forward. Grey had them ranged around the cabin, each moving forward on their own but ready to close up into a group should the man try to escape. He'll try to escape, thought Cassidy.

They were almost at the cabin. The man had unpacked the mule and had been busy inside. They saw the light and now it sounded as if he was preparing supper for himself.

He came out of the cabin. "What the? Who are you?" The man froze for a moment, then gave a shriek that pierced the silence and echoed around the hills.

The noise startled each one of them, and before they realized what he was doing, the man gave a nimble jump into the air and took off, racing between Sam and Grey. They didn't have a chance to stop him. They all whirled around and began chasing after him, but he drew a pistol and, half-turning, shot wildly again and again before running on. It was Tom who had been the quickest to react and was closing in on him. Another shot came from the man's gun.

Shot, Tom fell to the ground with a groan. Then the man turned around again. He fired, and this time Sam fell. A quick glance as she ran past satisfied Cassidy that Tom was hit in the shoulder and Sam in the leg. Not life-threatening.

A quick glance at Grey and she ran on, with him close beside her.

"Get ready to drop to the ground if he whirls around again," Grey whispered between panting breaths to Cassidy.

"Will do," was all Cassidy could manage, her breath coming in gasps as she ran forward after the fugitive.

They were uncertain how many bullets he had in the gun, and whether he had another. Still, they followed him. A disadvantage for them was that he knew the territory. He knew where he was going. They followed the figure in front of them, both determined to catch him.

As Cassidy drew a ragged breath, she thought about how he not only had the deaths of those innocent people on his hands but now he had injured two of her friends. "You will pay, you will pay," she vowed.

A sideways glance from Cassidy revealed the set face of Grey. Like her, he was still running at a steady pace after the fugitive. Neither she nor Grey was out of breath.

"He's fading, can't keep up the pace," muttered Grey to Cassidy. "Be ready to take him."

Cassidy didn't have any breath spare to reply. She hoped Grey saw her nod as she ran beside him. Tired and breathless, still they kept up with him and were even gaining.

Meanwhile, the sunlight was fading. The shadows on the far side of the canyon were lengthening and spreading long fingers of darkness across the landscape. Some of them were even reaching the middle of the canyon, beside the stream running alongside the path the fugitive had taken.

He fell. The cry of pain pierced the silence that hung over the canyon.

"Wait, Cassidy. He's an animal. Now he's a wounded animal. Take cover!" Grey flung himself down behind a boulder, pulling Cassidy beside him.

As she fell beside him, thunder reverberated around the canyon. The sun was obliterated, and an eerie half-light engulfed them as the clouds that had been threatening all afternoon bore down upon them.

Still, it didn't rain.

The noise of the thunder hid any movements of the fugitive.

"I'll go to the right, you to the left, Cassidy. But take care, Cassidy. Take care." He whispered these words in her ear and gripped her arm above the elbow, tightly. He looked into her violet eyes, which were staring at him. Lightning flashed around them and lit up their faces. Her wide-eyed wonder reflected in his eyes, his intent and brooding as he looked into her face, worry etched on his brow for her safety. As if emerging from a trance, he shook his head and whispered yet again, "Take care, Cassidy."

Ever afterward, Cassidy shuddered when she heard lightning come close. Echoing round and round again and again, thunder covered their approach toward the fugitive.

"There you are," she whispered to herself. A lightning flash lit up the surrounding scene. There, huddled beside a rock, he lay. Was he hurt? Or was he fooling them? Perhaps it was a ruse to get them up close so he could kill them both and free himself from their pursuit.

One step at a time; one silent step at a time. The words in Cassidy's brain drowned out the noise of the storm. The air about her was hot, heavy and humid. Unusual in the dry heat of the desert, the air hung heavily around her. It was becoming difficult to breathe. The atmosphere was loaded with the storm's vicious energy. Cassidy drew closer. She looked to the side and saw Grey, stooped, as he, too, took a slow step at a time.

Conscious of her gaze upon him, he cast a sideways look at her. His hand gave her a signal. Keep back, stay where you are.

Cassidy stopped where she was, moving only slightly to one side behind the cover of a large cactus. Taking a breath, she held it in and watched as Grey grew closer and closer to the man lying huddled on the ground.

This time, the lightning flashed in a brilliant sheet of

white. Cassidy closed her eyes tight. It almost hurt if she didn't shield them from the glare of that light.

Closer now. Grey was almost upon the man. His gun was at the ready. Only a few steps more.

CHAPTER TWENTY-FOUR

A rock flew through the air toward Grey. He ducked, and it missed him, giving the assailant time to sprint away into the shadows. He fled higher and higher alongside the stream that gushed down from the mountains.

"Are you all right?" Cassidy asked as she rushed to Grey's side.

"Yes, but he took me by surprise. Luckily, I dodged in time." He stood up, shook himself, and looked after the man. "I'm going after him, and I will catch him," he vowed.

A quick glance and he told Cassidy to stay. "You stay here or go back to the others. There is no need for you to come with me."

Cassidy thought of the poor young boy she had seen lying dead in the street and the wounding of Sam and Tom. "I'm coming. Let's go!"

The rain fell, not like normal rain but in sheets of enormous drops that blinded them. It lashed them and whirled around them. Still, they followed the man. He was slowing now, and the occasional looks he gave behind him showed his increasing terror at their continued chase.

Neither Grey nor Cassidy spoke. Side by side, they toiled up the perilous slope, the rain soaking into their clothes. The terrain shifted to rocks and gravel underfoot, and the scrubby undergrowth no longer slowed their progress. Now, it was the slipperiness of the rocks that posed the biggest problem.

"He's fallen!" Grey said, and they picked up their pace.

Closing the gap, it looked as if they might reach him.

But he rose to his feet and, seeing how close they were, took time to shoot at them.

"Down, Cassidy, down!" Grey, guessing that by the way the man stood that he was going to fire at them, threw himself and Cassidy flat on the ground. Not a moment too soon. The shots passed harmlessly over their heads.

"If you hadn't done that …" Cassidy muttered into his chest. His arm shielded her as they lay on the wet ground.

Raising his head, Grey peered to see what the killer was doing, only to find him running again, this time alongside the stream on a treacherously narrow path going upward.

"The stream—it's like a river, the water is rising," Cassidy noted, seeing the small stream growing into a raging torrent.

"It's the rain. This is a river like I've never seen before. There have been many storms over the last few days. This is the result." He grabbed her arm, pulling her away from the river.

Cassidy pushed the wet bonnet from over her eyes and looked after the fleeing man. "What are you doing, Grey? Aren't we going after him?"

"No need. We have to look out for ourselves. We need to get to higher ground."

The urgency in his voice and the panic in his eyes, visible in a flash of lightning, made her run to keep up with him. Clambering higher over the rock ledge, and then higher still, Grey struggled. Each time he climbed, he reached down and pulled her up to join him.

Finally, he stopped and looked around. "This'll do." It was a flat outcrop of rock with scraggly grass and a stunted tree. Behind them, the rock face soared up to form one peak of Devil's Mountain. "Sit down, Cassidy. We're wet, but we're safe."

"Look, I can see him. We're so high up, we can see him clambering up beside the river." The rain had lessened, and the menacing clouds had parted. Some still moved across the mountain tops, but others were lighter and drifted over them.

"The storm is passing. It's lighter now, even though it's getting late," Grey said. "Come here, Cassidy. We'll have to huddle together to keep warm. I hope you don't mind."

Uncertain whether or not she minded, Cassidy allowed herself to be pulled closer into his arms. After a few moments, his warmth thawed her frozen limbs, and she was grateful to feel safe and secure.

Cassidy jumped. "Is that more thunder? There are no strong clouds overhead now. Where's the thunder coming from?"

"That's not thunder; it's water. This stream becomes a river when it rains. Heavy rain pours down over the rock faces, and the only outlet is the stream. From the top of the mountain, it picks up more water as it comes downstream. Then it becomes a mighty flood, carrying everything before it. Look, our killer is in trouble."

Even the sun seemed delighted that the Pebble Killer was going to meet his end and shone on them all. Lit up in the last rays of the fading sun, Cassidy saw the man halt in his frantic scramble up the riverside. He stopped and looked up at the approaching wall of water. His screams could be heard from where they stood. Cassidy looked away. There was no way he didn't deserve his end, but she couldn't watch any man be swallowed up in the tumbling, roaring water.

Grey's arm tightened around her as the water reached their level. But he had chosen well, and it rushed beneath them.

Cassidy thought longingly of the oilcloth slicker sitting on the back of her horse. She was soaked through, the rain now cold and unrelenting, striking them with increasing force. Grey reached out and grabbed her hand to help her. It was time to return and catch up with Sam and Tom.

"There's no hurry now. Take your time and take care." Together, they stepped through puddles, slid across rocks, and retraced their steps down from where they had chased the fugitive. The noise of the river, swollen and raging alongside them, grew louder as they navigated the narrow path.

Cassidy knew this path was above the river's level, even in full flood. But for how much longer? She noticed the anxious sideway glances Grey gave it, and as the river's roar grew louder and it rose higher, he did not slow their pace.

"We've got to hurry, Cassidy. This is bad. It's the worst I've ever seen."

"Will Sam and Tom be safe? Are they above the level this water will reach?" Cassidy gasped, struggling to keep her footing on the slimy, wet rock. Grey shrugged his shoulders. But like her, he couldn't judge how high the cabin was or if it would be safe from the floodwaters.

Out of the canyon, now away from the narrow path, they still hurried to reach the two men. Both were anxious to see how badly they had been injured. The noise lessened as they moved away from the river, and the rain finally began to cease.

"Not much further now," Grey said encouragingly,

drawing Cassidy's wet hand through his arm as he helped her across a particularly nasty rocky outcrop.

"No, and it's much easier going down here. The rocks are fewer and less slippery," Cassidy panted, struggling to keep up with Grey.

"There it is. Look, there's the cabin, and the river still has some way to go before it will reach it. I think the old boy who built that cabin knew what he was doing."

The speed with which they had descended the mountainside away from the narrow gorge and its death trap of ferocious raging water had left them both exhausted. As they drew nearer to the cabin, Grey paused for a moment, trying to catch his breath, and pointed. "Look, there's smoke from the chimney. They must be all right."

His voice must have carried over the noise of the river and the gentle drizzle that was now falling.

The door of the cabin opened, and Cassidy saw Tom standing there, his arm bandaged up.

"Come on in, you both look like drowned rats. Get inside and dry off." Cassidy noticed Grey's attention was focused not on the cabin but on the covered lean-to. Standing beneath it, sheltered, were the horses and the supplies. Cassidy saw they had been fed and were now looking out at the rain.

"Sam—how is Sam? I saw the killer shoot him. Is he all right?" Cassidy's voice croaked as she staggered through the door. Her eyes brightened as she saw Sam sitting on a chair, a bandage around his calf.

"I'm fine. It was only a through and through," Sam replied. His shrewd eyes looked from one to the other, and he said, "The killer?"

Grey, now inside the door, flung off his jacket, the

soggy hat, and kicked off his boots. "Dead. The rising river water got him. The last we saw of him, he was tumbling head over heels down into a raging torrent. He'd have been dead in minutes."

Sam and Tom relaxed, letting out a big sigh of relief.

"Cassidy, I have your saddlebag here with your spare clothes in it. Go over to the far corner, strip off and change. Rub yourself dry with the blanket, then come over to the fire," Sam said.

The three men turned their backs to her. Tom poured out hot coffee for all of them and fiddled with an old frying pan on the stove, producing wonderful smells of bacon, beans and fried potatoes. "The killer had brought up plentiful supplies. I reckon he was gonna stay here for some time."

Cassidy stood for a moment, then swiftly divested herself of her sodden garments. Rubbing herself with the blanket, she draped it around her shoulders as she pulled on a dry change of clothes. It felt good to be dry, but she was still shivering. She made her way toward the fire.

"Here, sit close to it and take this coffee," said Grey. She noted he had changed as well, his long black hair, usually neat, now tousled and sticking up. His teeth chattered as he reached into his saddlebag for a bottle of brandy. Grey poured a generous tot into everyone's tin mug, but when Cassidy shook her head, he poured a tiny spot into her coffee. "You need it, Cassidy. You're suffering from shock, exhaustion, and a near-drowning in that rain."

Cassidy nodded and murmured her thanks. The fiery brew tingled on her tongue, the smell of the brandy strong. Unused to any alcohol, she had seen what it could do and feared losing control, so she rarely touched it. The warmth spreading through her was most welcome. She felt the chattering of her teeth slow down, her aching, leaden limbs growing warmer and more relaxed. The plateful of food passed over to her looked wonderful. Still seated by the fire, with the plate on her lap, she devoured it, feeling almost human again when she had finished.

Sam sat back, his injured leg sticking out in front of him. "What now?" The question hung amongst them, unanswered for a while. Their aim for some time had been to catch up with the killer. They had caught up with him, and now he was dead. What were they going to do next?

CHAPTER TWENTY-FIVE

The sky was clear, and moonlight bathed the pathway as they retraced their steps away from the cabin. It had been decided between them they would leave after they had eaten. None of them wished to spend the night in the killer's cabin. Knowing that it was going to be a moonlit night, they packed up after they had eaten, eager to get away from the oppressive atmosphere of the cabin and the sound of the flooding river. The silence of the night was broken only by the relentless roar of the river beside them.

Sam looked around, sniffed the air, and spoke with an urgency none of them had heard before. "We must hurry. More storms are coming. This may be our only chance to escape from Devil's Mountain. The next storm will be bad."

Cassidy thought they had been moving quickly before, but now they picked up the pace, their speed almost foolhardy on the slippery slopes they were descending. Despite the urgency, each step was taken with infinite care, ensuring their balance before continuing downward. Tom followed at the rear with the horses.

Grey, leading the way, turned and shouted back to Tom, "Leave the horses behind if they're difficult to manage. You're more important than the horses. Let them go if you have to save yourself."

The soft rain fell, and clouds gathered behind them. The journey seemed endless to Cassidy, a nightmare she couldn't wake from.

"This way!" Grey shouted, leading them down a narrow trail away from the river. Cassidy recognized their surroundings. They were approaching the valley and the tiny canyon where Martha and Reuben had made their camp. She hoped they were both sheltering in the cave. It had been weeks since she'd seen her friend Martha, and she hadn't looked well. Despite her assurances that she was happy and content with her new husband, Reuben, Cassidy was worried. Martha, a tall woman with broad shoulders, had always seemed larger than most men, but not Reuben. The stocky blacksmith was a giant, and they had found companionship with each other.

Martha had become Cassidy's maid and companion, hired after Cassidy's parents were murdered. Martha's face bore a twisted scar from forehead to chin, a cruel reminder of a violent past. Despite her hardships, Martha never spoke of them. A loving bond had grown between the two women, making them inseparable until Martha's marriage.

As if sensing Cassidy's worry, Grey turned and shouted, "Not long now, and the river hasn't risen too much here."

The moonlight, their longtime guide, now vanished behind clouds. The wind, which had calmed, was rising again, and Cassidy could almost feel the storm gathering strength.

"Reuben, Martha, are you here? It's Grey!" His shouts echoed around the tiny canyon, nearly drowned out by the river's roar.

Cassidy urged her horse past Sam, riding up to Grey as they approached the level ground around the cave. "Martha, it's Cassidy!"

A stocky figure appeared at the cave's mouth, shotgun in hand, and looked toward them. "Cassidy? Is that you? Cassidy!"

Jumping off her horse, Cassidy ran to embrace her

friend, fighting back tears. Martha was the one person left who understood and loved her. Cassidy vowed never again to leave it so long before seeing her friend.

As they drew apart, Cassidy's eyes widened at the sight of Martha's growing belly. "You're pregnant, Martha! How wonderful." She hugged her again, masking her dismay. How would they get Martha down the mountain quickly in this terrible weather?

Grey approached them. "Where's Reuben?"

Martha grabbed his arm, her voice urgent. "Find him, Sheriff. He left two days ago to pan for gold at a pool near a waterfall across the river. I haven't seen him since. You must find him."

The group exchanged worried glances. Panning beneath a waterfall was dangerous, especially with the river in tumultuous flow.

Martha sobbed quietly. "He has gold. Enough to live on for a while. I wanted to go back down to Nowhere, not stay here to have the baby alone. But all Reuben could think of was getting more gold. He has gold fever. He's gone mad with his love of gold."

Inside the cave, they warmed themselves by Martha's fire. Grey reached for the hot coffeepot on the embers. Martha busied herself, wiping away tears as she served them food and coffee. No one spoke, each casting anxious looks at the weather and listening to the ever-growing noise of the river.

Grey finished his coffee. "The journey down from here is tricky with horses. The narrow ledge will be slippery and dangerous. Leave most of the baggage here. Take only what you need to stay dry and warm. We need to go now. There's a break in the clouds but look over toward Devil's Mountain. The storm is gathering strength."

Martha stared at the sheriff. "What about Reuben?" Her hands twisted the edge of her shawl, the tassels becoming tangled in her fingers.

For years afterward, Cassidy would remember that moment. The smell of smoke from the fire, the constant roar of water, and Martha's tearful sobs. She put an arm around her friend, uncertain what to say.

"What about Reuben? We have to find him!"

CHAPTER TWENTY-SIX

Grey stepped forward and took Martha's fidgeting hands in his. "Martha, we can't look for him in this weather. What would he want you to do? What would he tell you and the baby to do now? We have to get to safety. Can you manage the narrow path down the cliff edge?" His calm, earnest voice reassured Martha.

She disappeared into the cave and returned with a canvas satchel across her body and an old coat of Reuben's draped over her shoulders. Cassidy knew she was saying goodbye to the cave, never to return. Martha looked around. Her gaze was sad, and Cassidy knew Martha would never set foot up here again. She had been weeping softly, but now she wiped her eyes with the back of her hand, gave a loud sniff and looked round at Cassidy. "Time to go."

Grey had been checking the horses, and in the cave-like stable that had been used by the old miner and Reuben for the horses, he found food for them, which he emptied.

"The pathway is wet and slippery, and the noise of the river rushing alongside it is going to spook the horses. But the mules will be fine. Now we have two, and they will carry Cassidy and Martha down the hill."

Both women protested, but Grey would have none of it. "You, Martha, need the security of the mule to take you down there. You are big now with child, and it would be difficult for you to keep your footing." Clutching her large belly, Martha could no longer disagree with him and had him help her up onto the mule.

Grey looked surprised when Cassidy protested. "Sam has a wound in the leg and Tom has a shoulder wound.

Sam should ride."

The mule was led out behind the one carrying Martha by Tom. "I'm fine, Cassidy, it's nothing."

Sam stood there and just shook his head.

Cassidy turned to Grey and before she knew what was happening, the powerful sheriff, with his two hands, hoisted her up on the mule. Cassidy glared down at him. "Exhaustion after that chase of ours, after the Pebble Killer does not make for a sure footing. And you, Cassidy, are exhausted!"

Cassidy opened her mouth to protest, but as she sat on the back of the mule she felt the ache in her bones flood over her and realized that he was correct. She had been too tired to clamber down that path. In fact, she knew her legs would not have carried her—they were utterly spent.

Never again did any of them speak of that journey. Rain swept over them in sheets, wind whistled around them, lashing the spiteful rain into their faces. The first treacherous path down the steep narrow path beside the cliff and rock face took everyone's grit and determination to manage it.

In single file, Sam led them down, clearing any fallen rocks that had fallen and posed an obstruction to those coming after him. Next came Martha. She had slumped down onto the mule and held the reins in one hand and with the other held the precious cargo in her stomach. She wondered at first whether she'd have to guide the mule, but there was no need. This sure-footed beast made his careful way down that path. Grey came next, between the two women. At first, he kept glancing back to check the sure-footedness of the mule that Cassidy was managing. But the mule did not bother about the gusts of wind, nor the incessant rain. He put his head down and cautiously trotted down the narrow path.

Cassidy at first clung tightly to the mule, but then realized it knew exactly what it was doing, and she spent the rest of the journey—after one horrified glance at the river beside her—with her eyes tightly shut.

"Now, we can relax a bit. The worst of the journey is over," Grey said as they reached the flatland of the canyon. The river was now some feet away from them and racing through a deeply carved rock formation. "But that river could flood higher at any moment, so we must hurry to reach the safety of Broken Horseshoe Ranch."

They were nearing the ranch when Tom put his fingers to his mouth and gave an ear-splitting whistle. It was almost dawn and the last few miles had been done with the fading of the surrounding darkness. The moon had lost its power to shine them on their way, but it was encouraging to each one of them to see the streaks of light appearing above Devil's Mountain.

The door of the ranch house was flung open and Chan stood there and gave an answering whistle. He and Ben tumbled down the steps and raced toward the bedraggled and weary travelers.

CHAPTER TWENTY-SEVEN

It was midday. Cassidy woke up in a room which was no more than a cupboard. The walls were papered with newspaper. She remembered Amy telling her about this bedroom, and she smiled as she stretched out. Warm and dry. It had been wonderful to fall into this bed after the care given to her by Nancy and Leah. After Martha, of course. The older woman in advanced stages of pregnancy had been cosseted by the two other women, Nancy, who had married the former owner Luke, and Leah, who had lived here for ages. Despite her protests, Martha had been placed in the big bed in which Luke had slept.

Cassidy reached for the cotton robe, which hung on a hook. Wrapping it around her, she pushed the door open and went out into the cabin itself. Only Nancy sat there, and she gave her a smile of welcome. "Come on, have a drink and something to eat. You slept well, didn't you? I looked in on you a few moments ago, and again earlier."

"Thank you, I am thirsty. How's Martha?" Cassidy said in between sips of coffee.

"She's fine. Exhausted, but still sleeping."

Wrapping the robe around her, Cassidy sat at the table. "What about the others?"

Pushing a plate of beans and bacon toward her, Nancy said, "Eat. It's just what everybody else had, eat it up. I will get you something better and tastier later on. Grey and Sam have gone into town. Tom is still here."

Cassidy finished eating, drank the coffee, and then stood up, lost in thought. "My clothes Nancy? I need them. I'm going to follow them into town. There are things I must do."

Nancy raised an eyebrow. "Can't you leave it to the men?"

An eyebrow was raised in return by Cassidy. "Would *you* leave it to the men?"

Nancy roared with laughter and slapped her thigh. "Well said, girl, well said!"

A short time later, the buggy left Broken Horseshoe Ranch with Ezra at the reins. Cassidy sat beside him. Martha had declared herself fit for travel. The slow pace of the buggy was not to Cassidy's liking, but she didn't want to demand a horse, and Nancy and Leah would not let her leave without an escort. Martha, who had insisted on joining her, because of her condition, had to sit in the buggy.

To her astonishment, Tom said he was going over to Dry Creek Ranch and there he would be staying.

"No more traveling around with you, Cassidy. I've been shot at and had the most horrendously awful time. I'm going to settle down and enjoy myself with a quiet life at Dry Creek Ranch."

His wound had been patched up and his arm wasn't too painful, the bullet only grazing it, but he made the most of his injury, wincing whenever he moved it. Cassidy wasn't fooled by this, but she understood that he'd had enough of excitement and was determined to live a more settled life. So here she was going to Nowhere with Ezra and Martha.

It was a silent trip back to Nowhere. Ezra was never one to chatter, and Martha and Cassidy had much process after the ordeal they had been through.

"Dora will be pleased to see you back, Martha. She was always asking after you," Cassidy said, attempting to lighten the mood.

Martha patted her tummy and replied, "She'll get a surprise when she sees me, won't she?"

They reached a crossroads. One track led to Dry Creek Ranch, the other into Nowhere. They took the Nowhere track, but further along there was a trail not much used that provided access to the wider country out West.

"Look over there! There are folks on the trail," said Ezra, pointing ahead to the seldom-used path.

All of them stared as Ezra drew the buggy to a halt. They could see individual riders, a couple of buggies, and even one or two wagons. All were moving at speed along the trail.

"Never seen that before. Can't work that out," said Ezra. He set off again, and all three of them stared, puzzled, at the increasing numbers on the track. As they turned onto the main track, the oncoming wagons, horses and buggies increased, advancing toward them.

"What the heck is the rush? Move over! Give a man some room!" Ezra shouted, exasperated at the constant flow of traffic and their complete disregard for him. He was constantly moving to the side of the track, sometimes coming to a complete halt as the travelers passed dangerously close to them. Ezra tried asking them what the rush was, but no one took the time to reply.

"What's happened in Nowhere?" Cassidy asked. "There's no smoke, so it can't be a fire. If it had been an earthquake, we would have felt it."

CHAPTER TWENTY-EIGHT

They reached the outlying districts of Nowhere, a newer part of the town built of shanties, lean-tos and tents, and were astonished at how much it had changed since their last visit.

"The canvas tents are gone. There's very little wood lying around. Maybe Manuel and Eliza can tell us what's going on," Cassidy suggested as they passed the normally bustling shanty town and turned into the general store's yard.

She helped Martha down from the buggy and left Ezra to see to his horse. Cassidy ran up the back steps of the general store and rushed inside, where she found Eliza. "What's going on? What's happened? We've seen everyone leaving town?"

Eliza stood there, looking out of the window. "Gold fever! They found gold over in those far mountains. And it's been proved there's no gold here. It was all a scam, a trick by that man, Oliver."

"Cassidy, come on in. Are you all right?" Eliza turned away from Cassidy and looked at Martha as she waddled up the last of the back steps into the store's back room. Eliza's eyes widened, her mouth forming a large "oh" before pouncing on Martha with an almighty hug. "You're pregnant! How wonderful! Come and sit down and tell me all about it."

Shaking her head at Eliza, Cassidy knew she would get nothing more from the woman now involved in baby talk with Martha. She smiled at Martha's face, which was full of happiness at Eliza's delight. Walking into the general store, she found Manuel at the doorway, watching as the township emptied.

"Is everybody going?" she asked as she came up behind him.

"Yes. I'd heard that a gold field town could turn into a deserted one when the gold ran out. Now, we're seeing it happen."

"Is it going to affect your trade, Manuel?" Cassidy asked the large proprietor as he stood there, his thumb hooked behind his braces, rocking backward and forward while watching the outgoing horses and buggies.

"Yes, but I was careful, Cassidy. I didn't expand too much. To tell the truth, it was exhausting. I've saved quite a bit and will be quite pleased to get back to my old customers and the usual routine.

"What about you, Cassidy? The Pebble Killer is dead, and that man Oliver is in jail. What will you do now?" His eyes twinkled at her, knowing her and her past exploits. "Going bounty hunting again?"

"Not sure, Manuel. Maybe I'll settle down and become a rancher."

His laughter followed her as she went back to see if Martha would accompany her to the hotel. The two women walked along the street. The township was emptying rapidly, and only a few people were on the boardwalk. They entered the hotel to be greeted by Dora, who exclaimed at the sight of Martha.

"My post?" Cassidy asked, breaking into the conversation.

"It arrived earlier," Dora replied, sparing a moment from the baby talk to tell her.

When Cassidy entered the front lobby of the hotel, she looked toward the table. The lobby in the hotel had been made into an imitation of a smart city hotel. Ornate decor had been added and the old frontier look when you entered the hotel was now gone. The table shipped from an eastern city was one of the newest additions. A large book, ready for guests signing into the hotel, sat beside a designated place for the post. Sometimes the post was sandy and even coffee-stained from its time spent in the wagon on the journey from Duloe to Nowhere.

Cassidy found several letters. She expected some from her lawyer, but it was the last one she picked up that puzzled her. Her name was printed in block letters on the envelope, which itself was grimy and stained. With a sense of foreboding, she struggled to open it using Dora's ornate gilt letter opener, that was placed beside the tray of letters. As she finally pried it open, a lock of hair tumbled onto the table. Her fingers trembled as she reached for it. Cassidy picked it up and studied it. Blond hair, unmistakably that of a young child. It lay in the palm of her hand in a golden curl.

Cassidy's hands shook as she unfolded the note that accompanied the hair. *"We have the man and the boy. Go to Duloe Boarding House. Wait for instructions if you ever want to see them alive again."* She sank down into the chair beside the table and read the words over and over. There was no mistaking that ominous threat. Josh and his son had been captured and were being held for ransom! She and the others waving Josh goodbye on his journey back to England had thought he was well on his way.

Cassidy's initial shock gave way to a cold, focused determination. She placed the note beside the envelope and looked at the lock of hair resting in her palm. Then, with a fierce resolve, she clenched her hand into a fist around the hair, her knuckles turning white. Anger surged through her veins like fire. She vowed not to rest until

Josh and his son were safely back.

Cassidy jumped to her feet, glancing around the hotel lobby. What should she do next? She had to consider the full implications of Josh's kidnap and not rush headlong into a foolish rescue attempt. What should she do?

CHAPTER TWENTY-NINE

The thought of young Charlie in the hands of some villain made her blood boil. He was such a tiny child, brought to America from England by his uncle, a wicked man who had been determined to kill his father, Josh. As the elder brother, Josh had been the rightful Lord of Ravenswood, a title his younger brother had long coveted. Many times, his younger brother had tried to kill him to seize the title, the grand house and the lands that came with it.

"Poor Josh," she murmured to herself, the lobby echoing her words. "Left for dead in the desert sun when Amy Tanner found him, barely alive." His memory had been shattered, and to this day he had never fully recovered it. Now, he had been kidnapped. All he had to his name when Amy found him was a small note hidden in his shoe with the words: "Josh Barnes. Go to Broken Horseshoe Ranch." That was his only link to his past life. Yet his past had caught up with him with the arrival of his son and his vengeful brother. But he could remember neither of them, nor the past life he had shared with them in England.

Shaking her head, Cassidy muttered, "I thought I could finally relax. After the gold fever troubles, I hoped my life would be quieter." Her voice, calm but steely, bounced off the walls of the empty lobby. She carefully placed the lock of hair back in the envelope and set it beside the threatening note. Her violet eyes, usually so soft, now burned with fierce resolve as she turned sharply and walked toward the door. Any hesitation she felt had vanished. Cassidy had made a promise. And Cassidy always kept her promises! "Josh, I'm coming. You and Charlie will be rescued, and soon!"

As she walked toward the door, she could hear the cheerful chatter from inside the room. Cassidy hated to break up their happiness, but there was no choice.

Following the recent flash floods, there was widespread damage and destruction. The raging torrents had wiped out the gold field diggings and swept down the foothills of Devil's Mountain. Much of the canyon where Martha and Reuben had been prospecting was flooded by the violent surge of water cascading down from the mountain. The storms had been relentless, and the floodwaters had devastated the landscape.

"I have to tell them, but I hate to upset Martha," Cassidy whispered as she paused outside the door. Inside, her companion, her former maid and now close friend, could be heard laughing. Reuben, Martha's new husband, had been lost in the flood. But even before that, he had been lost to the lure of gold fever. Heedless of Martha, he had searched for gold along the narrow creek in the canyon, neither eating, nor sleeping. His constant obsessive search was for gold. Martha was heavily pregnant, and as an older woman of considerable size, she was finding her pregnancy difficult. Martha had led a hard life, finding happiness late in life with Reuben. The large scar that ran from her forehead to her chin on one side of her face bore witness to the brutality of the life she had led. Losing her husband now seemed a cruel twist of fate. Now Cassidy had to break into that rare sound of laughter with more bad news.

Pushing the door open, Cassidy entered the room. The two women looked up at her, still laughing and smiling.

"What is it, Cassidy? What's wrong?" Dora, the hotel owner, sprang to her feet, her laughter fading away as she saw the grim determination and pallor on Cassidy's face.

"The post Curly brought up ...there was a letter," Cassidy said, holding up the letter. "It's a ransom demand. Someone has kidnapped Josh and little Charlie." Her voice was steady and cold, her previous moment of panic and indecision gone. Both women stared at Cassidy before exclaiming and swearing loud and long at her announcement.

Now the real Cassidy stood before them. A petite blonde with enchanting violet eyes and a trim figure, she usually dressed in stylishly cut outfits. Often she wore a man's denim shirt, a heavy cotton skirt, and flamboyant cowboy boots, completed by a fringed suede jacket. Cassidy looked like the picture of demure innocence, standing white-faced before them. But the women weren't fooled by her diminutive size and elegant appearance.

Dora, who now owned the hotel after the murder of her husband, had grown close to Cassidy. Martha, once employed as Cassidy's maid and now her trusted friend, also knew the real Cassidy. Despite her delicate looks, Cassidy was a stone-cold killer.

"I only kill the evil men, those who truly deserve it," she often said. Cassidy had a deadly skill with a knife, was proficient with a gun, and—thanks to her friend, Tom, the Chinese boy—had new skills in martial arts.

Cassidy was ready. Now she was going to find the kidnappers of Josh and Charlie. She could feel her resolve harden into steel.

"Let's prepare," she said, her voice like ice. "There isn't a moment to lose."

The room fell silent, the air thick with tension and determination. These two women knew what Cassidy was capable of and what she was willing to do to get Josh and

Charlie back. They had seen her in action and knew that as justice was always on her side; she always achieved her goal.

Cassidy, the stone-cold killer, was now was hunting for the kidnappers of Josh and Charlie. Seeing Cassidy's set and determined face, Martha almost felt sorry for the kidnappers. Almost. They now had Cassidy after them. Underestimated by every man who fell under the spell of her violet eyes, Cassidy was relentless in her pursuit. And always brought justice to the evil men on the Western frontier.

CHAPTER THIRTY

Martha and Dora read the letter and looked at the sad little curl of Charlie's hair. There was no hesitation from either of them.

"Cassidy, you must get them back safely," said Dora.

"Yes, and Cassidy, you must do whatever it takes to get them. I can't bear to think of the poor little boy in the clutches of some evil man," agreed Martha.

Cassidy gave them a wan smile at their vehement support for whatever action she needed to take. She raised a hand at both of them and then left the room, slipping out of the front door of the hotel and rushing toward the sheriff's office.

Despite her urgency, Cassidy paused for a moment and looked around in amazement. Another day, and Nowhere had changed yet again. The town was still emptying fast. The lure of the fortunes to be made from gold had brought thousands into the area. They had thronged the streets, filling any available space with lean-tos or tent-like homes made of canvas. A big hotel had sprung up overnight, built quickly from various tents and lumber. But now, everything had disappeared.

"Amazing, isn't it?" a voice came from behind her.

Recognizing him as one of the local men of the town, Cassidy could only reply, "Yes, it's all changing so quickly. Nowhere seems as if it's disappearing."

"I've been around a bit. Was in a town over California way after the gold rush there. It mushroomed and grew up with thousands in a matter of days." The elderly man spread his arms wide and shook his head. "Seen this happen as well. When the gold finished, the town was empty and deserted in a couple of weeks."

"It only took a couple of weeks?" Cassidy said, astonished. But looking up and down Main Street and the now almost empty sidewalks, she could believe it. "What happened to the town, then?"

"It died. That's what will happen to Nowhere," the old man said, shaking his head as he walked on.

"I hope not. I'd hate Nowhere to die," Cassidy replied.

With one last look down the emptying Main Street, Cassidy continued her hurried journey to the sheriff's office. Sheriff Lance Grey of Nowhere had arrived in town as a preacher. No one knew his backstory, and they didn't dare ask him. A tall, imposing figure with long black hair, he always wore black. No matter how hot it was, he always wore a flowing black coat, far too long for him. He could often be seen dashing down Main Street, the coat flowing behind him. Known for his fairness and honesty, Grey's mysterious past only added to his appeal among the people of Nowhere. He disliked his given name, Lance, preferring to be called Grey.

Pushing open the door to the sheriff's office, Cassidy remembered not to shove it back against the wall. Her habit had caused a large dent on the wall and regularly annoyed Grey.

"Cassidy—coffee?" Standing at the stove with his coffeepot in hand, Sheriff Lance Grey looked at the beautiful woman standing in his doorway and gave her his long, slow, lazy smile. "What now, Cassidy? Killed another bounty hunter? Knifed someone else to keep from being bored?"

At the stricken look on her face, he slammed the coffeepot down on the stove and strode toward her. "What's wrong, Cassidy? What is it?"

Wordlessly, she handed him the envelope. Without

looking at him as he read it, she walked over to the coffeepot and poured herself a small amount into a tin mug. She put it to her lips, grimacing at the harsh, strong brew that he always favored, and took a sip.

"When did this arrive? How did it get here?" Grey demanded.

"Curly brings the post from the wagon from Duloe each morning to the hotel."

"His free breakfast," murmured Grey. He knew the delivery of the post to the hotel was a ruse by Curly to get a free breakfast each morning. Dora, pleased to get the early mail delivered for her customers, was quite willing to give him breakfast.

"This was slipped between a couple of envelopes from my lawyers. I don't know how Curly came by it. I came straight to you." Again, she sipped a little of the coffee.

"Is this the boy's hair?"

Cassidy looked at the sad little lock of hair in Grey's large hand and nodded. She struggled hard not to cry when she thought of the little boy in the hands of some villain. He had been through so much. His mother had died at his birth, and his father, Josh, had been taken from England, beaten up, and left for dead in the Arizona desert. Josh had lost his memory and had only just been reunited with his son.

"Yes, that's his hair. He only met his father a few days ago. I can't imagine what that poor child is going through. He was being looked after by Ruth, who had worked at the hotel they were staying in. I wonder if she is with them? They don't mention Ruth. I hope she's not been hurt."

"The first thing to do is to speak to Curly, find out where this came from. The note says they'll contact you again about where to leave the gold. Do you have enough gold to pay for this amount they are asking for?" Grey asked as he walked back to the table and picked up his coffee mug. He drained it. "You know, they could already be dead." His voice was solemn and his intent look at the young woman betrayed sympathy for her, but he felt he needed to state the plain facts of the situation.

"I know," Cassidy replied, her voice steady but her eyes flashing with determination. "But I won't accept that until I see it for myself. I know we need to act quickly."

Grey nodded. "All right. Let's go find Curly. The sooner we get answers, the sooner we can get on their trail."

Cassidy set her mug down and followed Grey out the door. They made their way through the almost deserted streets of Nowhere, past abandoned tents and makeshift homes, to the small, ramshackle livery stable where Curly usually lingered.

Curly, a wiry man with a constantly nervous expression, looked up as they approached. "Sheriff, Miss Cassidy, what brings you here?" he asked, his voice quavering slightly.

"Curly, we need to know about this letter," Grey said, holding up the envelope. "How did it get into the post?"

The man's eyes widened as he recognized the envelope. "I … I don't know exactly. I just found it with the rest of the mail. I swear, I don't know who put it there."

"Think carefully, Curly," Cassidy urged, her voice calm but insistent. "Did you see anyone unusual hanging around the postbag when you collected the mail in Duloe?"

Curly furrowed his brow, clearly struggling to recall.

"Well, now that you mention it, there *was* a man I didn't recognise. He was hanging around, but I thought he was just another drifter looking for work."

"What did he look like?" Grey asked.

"Tall, with a scruffy beard and a worn-out hat. Didn't get a good look at his face," Curly replied.

Cassidy and Grey exchanged a glance. It wasn't much to go on, but it was a start. "Thank you," Grey said. "If you see him again, let us know immediately."

With that, they moved away from Curly, both of them deep in thought. "We need to find this man," Cassidy said. "He could lead us to the kidnappers."

Grey nodded. "We'll start by asking around Duloe Town. Someone else might have seen him. We need to go there immediately."

Cassidy's mind raced with possibilities. They had to hurry. Time was running out for Josh and Charlie, and she wouldn't rest until they were safe.

Both left the livery stable, returning to pack and hurry back in order to reach Duloe in time to receive the ransom note and save Josh and Charlie.

CHAPTER THIRTY-ONE

At the livery stable, Cassidy stood with her small carpetbag, waiting for Grey to join her.

"Cassidy! What are you doing here?" Tom, the young Chinese boy who should have been at Dry Creek Ranch, had ridden into the stable yard. Getting down off his horse, he walked over toward her.

"What are *you* doing here, Tom?" she asked in return. "Oh, Tom! It's the little Chinese girl, isn't it? What are you going to do about her?"

The last time she and Tom had been in Duloe, they had eaten at a small cafe where a young Chinese girl had tried, and failed, to be a server. Tom's younger brother, Chan, had also been forced to work in a hotel kitchen, where his clumsiness had got him thrown out. Both boys had been sold to America by their Chinese uncle. Tom feared this had happened to the girl.

"You think the Chinese girl has been bought and forced into work?" she murmured.

"Yes, I'm sure of it. But I need to go. Perhaps try to ask her." Tom secured his horse while they talked and came to stand beside her. He didn't look up but poked the dirt with his toe, examining it with great interest. Tom didn't know what he could do to help the girl, but he had to try.

"I'll come with you. If she's in trouble and has been bought by that man running the cafe, I'll see if we can buy her from him," Cassidy said quietly, putting a gentle hand on the boy's arm. "But I have to go to Duloe. Josh and Charlie have been kidnapped! They are demanding a ransom from me. I'm going to get a letter from them at the Duloe boarding house. I must finish my business there first. We can deal with the girl and rescue her afterward."

"We all thought Charlie and Josh were well on their way to England. Do you know when they were kidnapped? This is dreadful. I'll help you. What can I do Cassidy?"

Tom agreed with Cassidy after she explained why she was going to Duloe. "We must hurry, Cassidy," he said. "Time is running out for everyone, Josh, and Charlie and the little Chinese girl."

Cassidy nodded, her violet eyes burning with resolve. "Let's go, Tom. We have much to do."

"I can help you," Tom said earnestly. "Josh has been good to me, and he's had enough trouble without this. We can rescue him and his son first, then deal with the girl afterward." His determined expression made Cassidy smile. She was glad to have his company. Young and small he might be, but Tom possessed martial arts skills that could take most Western men by surprise. He had been practising his gunplay with Amy, and Cassidy herself had been teaching him how to throw a knife with precision.

"That would be good, Tom. I'll be pleased to have you along," she replied warmly.

***

Meanwhile, in the sheriff's office, the new deputy stood watching his boss. He wasn't inexperienced. He had served as a deputy in another small town further east. But he knew this place was far different from the sleepy town he had left behind. That town had bored him with its quiet monotony. Here in Nowhere, with all its chaos and lawlessness, he found life far more interesting, especially under the leadership of Sheriff Lance Grey.

Grey lifted his saddlebags and slung them over his shoulder, striding out of the sheriff's office toward the livery stable. As he got closer, he saw Cassidy. Her blonde hair was unmistakable as she stood talking to young Tom. She appeared delicate and fragile, her petite frame almost dwarfed by the young man beside her. But Grey knew better. He knew how powerful she could be, thanks to the martial arts skills Tom had taught her. And her skill with a knife was unparalleled. He would bet that many a man would fall short of her ability. Grey felt a certain wariness around Cassidy. He understood what drove her, in her thirst for justice and her relentless pursuit of bounty hunting. But he also sensed a vulnerability within her, a vulnerability that only fuelled his own attraction to her. That attraction worried him. Cassidy was not the kind of woman to get involved with lightly. Grey felt that Cassidy was not the kind of woman to get involved with at all!

The wagon was due to leave for Duloe. Two large women climbed aboard and took their places. Cassidy was about to board when she saw Grey, and also Sam, approaching. They both walked up to her and Tom.

Josh had made a friend in the half-Indian Sam, saving his and his family's life on occasions. Sam had also helped Josh and Amy from the Broken Creek Ranch survive villainous attacks. A strong bond had grown up between them. Grey had met Sam on Main Street and told him about the kidnap of Josh and Charlie.

"Sam is going to join us in our rescue of Josh," said Grey.

Cassidy was delighted to see the powerful Sam join them.

"Are you coming on the wagon?" she asked them.

Both men shook their heads. "We'll be riding," Grey said. "We'll meet you at the boarding house in Duloe. Are you riding, Tom?"

"I haven't got a horse," Tom replied.

"Let's get you a horse, and you can ride along with us," Sam suggested, smiling at the young man.

Cassidy watched as they saddled up their horses. She longed to join them, but young women were discouraged from riding alone or with men. They were expected to take the wagon to Duloe. The ride promised to be long, hot and dusty, and Cassidy could already tell it would be far from enjoyable, especially as a large, middle-aged couple squeezed onto the bench beside her. Cassidy sighed, but her outfit was not suitable for horse-riding. Dressed in an elegant costume of sage green, with intricate embroidered details on the cuffs and lapels, tiny leather boots and her newest bonnet, she would hate to get her new outfit ruined on a hot, dusty ride.

When she got down from the wagon in Duloe, Cassidy noticed that the gold rush that had fizzled out in Nowhere had also affected Duloe, though not as severely. The small town was still bustling, but the boisterous, gold-mad crowd that had once flooded in, eager to get to the Nowhere gold fields, had dissipated. On entering the boarding house, which had once been packed with people, Cassidy saw it was now quieter. The dining room, which used to be filled with benches crammed beside long tables, had returned to its previous tidy arrangement of small tables. A new owner greeted her, dressed impeccably and with her hair neatly arranged in a bun. Cassidy smiled, remembering the cheerful, dishevelled woman who had run the place during the gold rush frenzy.

"It's quieter in here," Cassidy commented.

"Back to normal," the owner replied. "The last woman made money when the rush of people flooded in here. She left, leaving the place a complete mess. She couldn't cope with so many staff and so many people."

Cassidy smiled and thanked her for the key. As she picked up her carpetbag and turned away, the owner gave her a strange smile and handed her an envelope. "This came for you today. Someone must have known you were coming."

Envelope in one hand, carpetbag in the other, Cassidy walked up the stairs to a room at the front. It was the same room she had slept in before. The window opened onto the flat roof of the porch, a feature Cassidy had made good use of many times. She flung the carpetbag onto the bed, shrugged out of her coat and moved to the window, where the light was better. She opened the envelope.

"Come out to the Lightning Tree this evening at 9 p.m. Bring the gold. The exchange will be made then."

Cassidy tossed the letter onto the dressing table and stood looking out over Main Street. She saw nothing, Too deep in thought, she saw nothing. Folding her arms, she muttered, "Stupid—they must think I'm stupid. To ride on my own at night to a certain ambush, carrying a bag of gold."

What if they didn't have Josh or the boy? What if it was a trap? It could be anybody's lock of hair. But deep in her heart, Cassidy knew it wasn't. That was a lock of hair from young Charlie. She glanced over at the letter again and wondered how to solve this problem. There was no way to reach the kidnappers. There was no way to refuse to turn up. She didn't know where the lightning tree was. She'd have to find that out. Cassidy felt an unusual sensation, one that she rarely had in her life. It was a feeling of uncertainty. And Cassidy did not like that feeling.

Cassidy paced the room, her mind racing. There had to be a way to outsmart these kidnappers. She needed a plan. And she needed it fast. Time was running out, and every moment she hesitated was a moment Josh and Charlie were in danger. She couldn't allow herself to fail. Not now. Not with those precious lives at stake.

CHAPTER THIRTY-TWO

A knock at the door broke her concentration. "Cassidy, it's Grey," came the sheriff's deep voice from the other side. "We need to talk."

Cassidy took a deep breath, steeling herself. "Come in, Grey," she called, her voice steady, betraying none of the turmoil inside her. She would figure this out. She had to. For Josh. For Charlie.

Grey entered, his face serious. "We've got a lot to discuss," he said, holding her gaze.

Picking up the letter from the dressing table, Cassidy silently handed it to Grey. "Read this letter. We need to figure out how to handle this meeting at the lightning tree."

Grey nodded, his expression hardening with resolve. "We need a plan," he agreed. "A plan that will ensure we get Josh and Charlie back safely. And we need to be ready for anything."

Grey handed back the letter and walked to the door. "I'll get Tom and a couple of others to help us. We'll be ready."

Cassidy watched him leave, then turned back to the window. She clenched her fists, her jaw set in determination. Tonight, they would face whatever was waiting for them at the lightning tree. And they would bring Josh and Charlie home.

Cassidy stood, undecided. It was many hours until she had to be at the drop spot for the ransom. A lot of time to fill. She knew Grey and Sam would be down at the livery stable, while Tom had already headed to the cafe to gather information about the Chinese girl.

That's it, Cassidy thought. Focus on getting the

Chinese girl away from her slavery in that dreadful cafe. Throwing on a coat, making sure she had all her weapons handy, she slipped out of the boarding house unobserved.

Cassidy turned toward the livery stables, hurrying toward them, and was relieved to see Sam and Grey emerging from them.

"Where is this lightning tree?" Grey was asking Sam, who shook his head, showing he hadn't heard of it either.

One of the young stable boys came out carrying a bucket and spade. Grey called out to him, "Hey, do you know where the Lightning Tree is?"

After a lengthy explanation from the boy, they realised the Lightning Tree was quite a distance from town, along a secluded stretch of road. There was no chance anyone could approach unnoticed. The kidnappers had picked the ideal spot. They were in control of the situation.

"You can't go alone," Grey said to Cassidy.

"What else can I do?" Her voice was flat, almost unnatural. She knew the danger she would be in if she went alone to meet them. They could easily kill her, take the gold, and no one would be the wiser. Worse, she could end up joining the hostages, adding another to their ransom demands.

Before they could discuss it further, they noticed Tom hurrying toward them. "It's more urgent than I thought," he said breathlessly. "Lee, that's her name. She whispered her name to me and told me she was going to be sent tonight to a brothel in the next town. She is no good at serving, so they have sold her on." Tom's voice faded, the horror of the situation rendering him speechless.

"So, she will be taken from the cafe tonight?" Grey asked, trying to make sense of Tom's rushed explanation.

"Yes, someone should arrive on the next stage. Then

she will be moved to the big town."

Tom looked distraught at this new information from the young girl, and Cassidy could see why. It was time to take action, she thought.

"Let's have a drink or a meal there right now," Cassidy suggested. "Not you, Tom. You should go to the livery stables and order a buggy and an extra horse. Have them readied in the next few minutes."

Cassidy glanced at Grey. His face was serious, but his eyes sparkled with a familiar gleam. He had a plan. She considered asking him about it, but decided against it. He would reveal it when he was ready.

The cafe was bustling with the last of the lunchtime crowd. Pushing open the door, Cassidy and Grey were hit by a steamy mixture of smells. The wooden shack had many tables set out and most were full. Cassidy was surprised to see the variety of customers. There were workmen still clad in dungarees or work clothes dropping in for a quick lunch. Well-dressed couples sat together, and beside the only empty table sat two extremely large ladies who were tucking into heavily laden plates. Behind them sat a well-dressed couple, talking earnestly to each other over the plates in front of them.

The tiny Chinese girl worked hard. Cassidy could see that she was still clumsy and struggling with the heavy plates and dishes. She kept glancing at the door, her eyes filled with a mix of hope and fear. Cassidy was glad Tom had stayed away. His presence might have made her reaction to the young Chinese boy too obvious. Tom's whispered conversation with the girl had aroused hope within her. Cassidy was determined that she would take her from this drudgery and the fear that consumed her.

Grey ordered the meal for both of them. Cassidy

couldn't care less what she was given. Her appetite had deserted her. The forthcoming meeting at the lightning tree was heavy upon her mind.

"You must eat something, Cassidy, you need it!" Grey said to her. "You need to keep your strength up, otherwise you lose your concentration and that edge you need."

The meal was adequate, though Cassidy found the greasy, watery gravy unappetizing. She picked at her plate, giving her hands something to do, and also because Grey expected her to eat. The mouthfuls she swallowed made her feel better. But she would never admit that to Grey.

Cassidy was about to speak to Grey when she noticed a large man enter. His clothes were travel-worn, and his face was hard, with empty eyes that scanned the room, assessing each person. He was followed by a large woman. Straight black hair swept back revealed a hard featured face with narrow lips and hooded eyes. She stomped into the cafe, her sharp eyes fixing upon the tiny figure of Lee. There was no doubt in Cassidy's mind as to why this woman had arrived at the cafe and who she had come for. There was no time to waste. They had to act. And act now!

CHAPTER THIRTY-THREE

Grey tensed beside Cassidy, as he watched the newcomers push past those already seated.

The wooden boards, ingrained with spilled grease from the fried bacon and other meats, potatoes, and biscuits, squeaked as Cassidy moved her chair back. Somehow, the noise and smells of the cafe crowded in on her. Overwhelmed by the hubbub, she fought to bring her thoughts back to the problem they now faced.

The tiny figure of Lee was close to them. Carrying a large dish of stew, she struggled toward the table at which the couple sat. Cassidy thought the girl looked no more than thirteen years old, although Tom said she was older. She knew the girl, pale-faced and thin, had to be rescued now.

Cassidy saw Grey shift in his chair toward Lee, and could sense he was working out a rescue plan. "Now would be the best time to grab her," he whispered. "Can you create a diversion?"

As the girl approached their table, threading her way through the crowded cafe, Cassidy deliberately dropped her spoon. It made a loud clatter on the floor beside her. With a loud exclamation, she rose from her chair and pretended to search for it underneath the table. Cassidy darted underneath the table and pinched the bottom, hard, of one of the large ladies seated nearby. In a second, she had returned to her place as the outraged woman jumped to her feet with a loud cry.

Turning to the man behind her, she shouted. "How dare you! Madam, your husband pinched my bottom!" she shrieked in a high-pitched voice. At her shout, the man had turned in his chair to look at her. The outraged woman flew at the elderly man seated behind her and slapped him across the face. He toppled backward, his chair breaking under his sudden shift in weight. The noisy commotion caused a domino effect. Diners rose to their feet to look at the disturbance.

"I didn't touch you! I wouldn't want to touch your butt!" the elderly man shouted back in denial. Uproar ensued as other people became embroiled in the argument.

In the confusion, Grey and Cassidy seized the moment of uproar and mayhem. Cassidy jumped to her feet and in seconds had reached Lee and grabbing her by the hand, she pushed her in front of her toward the door.

The large woman, realising the girl was being abducted, pulled out a gun. Cassidy screamed, "Gunfight! Everyone take cover!" Her shouts and yells added to the confusion and set off a wave of panic. Those nearest the woman with the gun screamed and scattered, rushing for the exit. In the chaos, Grey rushed the woman with the gun, snatching it from her. Moments later, and to his delight, the woman was knocked to the floor by the stampede of diners rushing past her toward the door.

"Hurry, this is our one chance. We must escape now!" Cassidy said to the girl.

The girl didn't hesitate, slipping through the crowd and exiting the doorway, Cassidy close on her heels. Outside they didn't draw breath, Cassidy urging the girl onward. Grey ran out of the diner behind her.

They ran through alleys behind a parade of makeshift shops and offices. Tom, who had been waiting, waved to the Chinese girl. Seeing him, she sprinted toward him. Cassidy caught up, and the four of them ran toward the livery stables.

The buggy was ready and waiting outside. Lee was bundled into it and covered with blankets and boxes.

"Keep quiet, no matter what you hear. We are taking you to safety," Tom reassured her.

Tom climbed onto the buggy and set off down the road toward the Dry Creek Ranch. Sam, who had been waiting at the livery stables, mounted another horse and followed.

"I'll make sure they're on the road to safety before I return," he called back to Cassidy.

Grey put an arm around Cassidy's shoulders, laughing. "That was brilliant, Cassidy. I knew you were resourceful, but I never imagined you could cause such a scene with one pinch!"

They laughed together as they walked back to the boarding house, but Grey soon turned serious. "Now, we need to plan tonight carefully. I don't want any of us getting killed."

CHAPTER THIRTY-FOUR

Grey paced up and down the small guest room of the boarding house, frustration etched on his face. He and Cassidy had been talking in circles for what felt like hours. Cassidy sat on the bed, watching him. The one chair in the bare room she'd left for him to sit in. Unable to relax, he had stomped around it. His eventual plan was to follow Cassidy at a distance, keeping to the shadows as she went to deliver the ransom. The plan was far from ideal, but it was the best he could think of in the difficult circumstances. The ransom drop had placed Cassidy at a meeting place and put her in a dangerous and vulnerable position.

Not long after, there was a knock at the window. Grey rushed to open it when he saw Sam standing on the flat roof of the porch.

"Cassidy, the sheriff is acceptable in your room, but as an Apache half-breed, I'm not. That's why I've come to the window," Sam explained.

"What about Lee and Tom?" Cassidy asked him. She got off the bed now, and went to the window, eager to hear how they had got on with the journey.

"They should be nearly at Dry Creek Ranch by now," Sam said. "I asked a couple of friends to escort them all the way there, just to make sure they arrived safely."

Sam's friends were from his tribal community. Some had chosen not to live on the reservation, instead integrating themselves by working on local ranches or carving out a precarious living in the mountains.

"Some other friends are already in position around the lightning tree," Sam continued, a pleased smile spreading across his face. His smile turned into a grin when he saw the expressions on Cassidy's and Grey's faces.

Grey, who had stopped pacing when Sam entered, now sank into the bed, staring intently at Sam. "Already in place?" he repeated, almost disbelieving.

"Yes," Sam confirmed. "Three of my best friends are there, keeping watch."

Grey's face softened with visible relief. "Well done, Sam. You've no idea how much better that makes me feel. I was going crazy trying to think of a way to secure the ransom drop and keep Cassidy safe without drawing attention to myself."

"Now you can stop wearing out the carpet, Grey," Cassidy said. She added, with a small, hopeful smile, "Let's trust that Sam's plan will work."

"Thank you, Sam," Grey said, his voice quieter now. That was all he said, but both Sam and Cassidy knew from the depth in his voice how much he meant it.

The hours dragged slowly as the clock ticked closer to nine. Grey retired to his room. There was no point in continuing to go over the plan; it would only heighten their nerves. Sam left to take his position near the lightning tree, hiding himself to watch over Cassidy's journey.

The sun was setting as Cassidy rode out, its golden glow stretching across the desert landscape. Despite the unusual warmth of the evening, an icy fear gripped her. Cassidy had faced danger before—many times—but this was different. This was a deliberate journey into a trap, a situation she knew was almost impossible to escape from if things went wrong. But she couldn't refuse to go. Josh had been a good friend, and loyalty demanded that she try. And there was Charlie. The little boy had been unnaturally solemn when she met him. Bewildered by the journey to America with an unfeeling and uncaring uncle and then presented to a father that he never knew existed, he had withdrawn within himself.

As Cassidy rode, her thoughts drifted to Josh. Their relationship had never gone beyond friendship. There had been a fleeting moment when she considered the possibility of something more, but Cassidy valued him too much as a friend. His openness, his uncomplicated nature, meant it was almost like having a kindly, protective brother.

The gold, in a small but heavy bag secured in front of Cassidy, was the ransom they demanded. No more, no less. Cassidy hated giving it up. It had been earned through hard gruelling work, and difficult hunts after evil men for bounty. As a woman without a husband or inheritance, she had learned early the value of financial independence. That gold represented freedom and security. Yet here she was, risking it all for a friend.

Cassidy drove the buggy with a steady hand, acutely aware of the weight of her skirt as it brushed against her legs. The outfit she chose that evening was not mere happenstance; it was a calculated decision. Her skirt concealed two hidden pockets. One held a knife, the other a small but deadly gun. Her jacket, buttoned tightly at the waist, featured a concealed pocket in the sleeve that housed a tiny pearl-handled revolver. It had been an extravagant purchase that had proven its worth on more than one occasion. This gun, light and easily manoeuvrable, could be swiftly deployed with a practiced flick of her wrist, catching many an unsuspecting foe off guard. Cassidy was no fool. She knew all too well that her precautions might count for nothing. A single, well-aimed bullet could render her skills useless the moment she came into view.

The sky was dimming, the last vestiges of daylight giving way to the encroaching shadows of twilight. The surrounding landscape darkened, with deeper shades lurking behind the scattered rocks, cacti and stunted trees that dotted the desolate track leading to the rendezvous point.

Ahead, the ground began to rise slightly, and at its summit stood a lone, gnarled, and twisted tree.

CHAPTER THIRTY-FIVE

As she had prepared to embark on this treacherous journey to deliver the ransom, Cassidy had descended the stairs of the boarding house with a sense of unease. Before leaving the bedroom, she looked round, checking that she had everything she needed. She closed the door behind her and wondered if she would ever see that room again.

The landlady had lingered in the hallway, offering a smile that seemed friendly enough but carried a hint of something else, an unsettling awareness that put Cassidy on edge. Cassidy had the feeling that she was in on the ransom plot and that she knew where Cassidy was going.

Yet, it wasn't the strange landlady's smile that occupied Cassidy's thoughts now: it was the shadowy figure she had glimpsed slipping hastily through a doorway at the end of the hall. The swift departure had immediately struck her as suspicious. And then Cassidy realized: she recognized that figure. A fleeting glimpse, but more than enough to stir something deep in her memory.

"Ruth!" The name surfaced in her mind like a bolt of lightning. Ruth, the cook who had charmed young Charlie at the hotel and whom Josh had employed as a nanny for their voyage to England. Ruth, who had seemed so warm and motherly, so utterly transparent in her affections for the young motherless boy.

"How could you betray us?" Cassidy muttered under her breath, her voice low but filled with a simmering anger as she drove on. "You gained that child's trust, acted as his rock in a world so foreign and desolate." Words flooded her mind, harsh and unforgiving words that her mother would never have approved of, not even in thought. Words that perhaps her mother didn't even know existed. The anger inside Cassidy flared, hot and fierce, but she welcomed it. It was better than the cold, paralysing fear that had threatened to engulf her. Anger could be harnessed, sharpened, used to keep her focused. As long as it did not overwhelm her.

***

It was the only tall feature in the flat, barren landscape, a slight rise in the ground leading up to the hill. The perfect vantage point for a kidnapper to survey the area, checking that she had come alone. A small cluster of rocks near the tree was shrouded in darkness, but as she approached she saw figures emerge, stepping forward from the shadows into the fading light.

Cassidy tightened her grip on the reins, drawing a deep, calming breath. This was no time for panic. She had to be vigilant, her senses razor-sharp. She squinted in the twilight and looked closer at the men.

Amongst the group, she saw a smaller figure. That had to be Charlie. He stood beside one man. Josh was kept apart from him beside another man, whom Cassidy assumed was the leader. Relief mixed with fear. They had brought the boy and Josh. But would they honor their end of the bargain? At the moment, she had ridden up toward them and she was unharmed. One hand slid into the pocket where she kept the gun. It felt comforting to her touch.

One man stepped forward, a self-assured swagger in his gait, and Cassidy brought the buggy to a halt. She had been correct at first glance. This man had to be the leader of the group.

"Do you have the gold?" he demanded.

Cassidy held up the bag, deliberately keeping herself at a distance. "Do you have Josh and Charlie? I need to see them." She *could* see them, but she wanted them pushed forward nearer to her.

The leader shoved Josh forward. His hands were tied behind his back, and Cassidy could see even in the dim light that his face was bruised and his lip had been bleeding. The boy was pushed forward and reached out to his father. Charlie clung to his side, gripping his trouser leg.

"We have them," the man said, gesturing behind him. "Throw the gold over, and you can have them in return."

"Bring them closer to the buggy first," Cassidy insisted.

The leader signalled for Josh and Charlie to be brought forward, but the second man, standing stiffly back, shook his head. He reached out a hand as if to grab Josh and pull him back.

"We'd be fools to hand them over now!" the second man shouted. "We take the gold and the woman. There is no one with her. No one will know what happened to her. With three hostages, we can demand even more gold!"

"Don't be more of a fool than you already are," the leader snapped. "We're in enough trouble as it is. Adding another hostage would only make things worse."

"I don't agree," the second man retorted, his tone belligerent. "I want the gold *and* the woman." He yanked Josh back just as Charlie took a step forward.

The leader grabbed Charlie and pushed him toward the buggy. "Give me the gold now," he ordered Cassidy. "You've got the boy." The leader motioned for the second man to bring Josh forward. But the second man rushed forward, reached out, and snatched the gold from

Cassidy's hand.

Cassidy leaned down to pull Charlie up beside her in the buggy. He scrambled up beside her, and she pushed him down to the floor at her feet for safety.

The second man abruptly shoved Josh to the ground, drew his gun, and fired at his leader. The man who had been leading both of them turned in horror as a bullet hit his shoulder. Before he could speak, another bullet ripped into him and he fell dead on the ground. The gold coins fell in a glittering shower from his grasp.

Seeing this, the second man hurriedly knelt down to retrieve the gold. Josh, struggling to get up from the ground with his hands tied, shouted at her. "Go, Cassidy! Take Charlie and go!"

CHAPTER THIRTY-SIX

Cassidy took the reins and urged her horse into a swift turn. She made a wide circle in an attempt for Josh to jump up as she passed. But gunshots rang out. The killer stood over his fallen comrade. The gold bag was now tied up and secured at his feet.

Before Cassidy could reach Josh, the man had grabbed him. He yanked Josh up to his feet with one hand. He pulled Josh in front of him and used him as a human shield, his gun pointed at Josh's head.

Cassidy sensed rather than saw the hidden presence of the Indians she knew were watching from the shadows, but they, too, could do nothing, with Josh held with a gun at his head.

"Go, Cassidy!" Josh's voice was resolute, almost commanding. "Take Charlie to safety. Go, Cassidy!"

With a final glance back at the captive Josh, her heart heavy, Cassidy turned the buggy and sped off into the gathering darkness. Her back felt itchy as she turned it away from the man. A bullet in her back could hit her at any moment. Would he shoot her? Or would he leave her and demand yet more ransom gold from her for Josh's safe release?

Charlie clung to her skirt as she careered down the rough track. She had little time to spare for the child. Cassidy knew she had to get away from the man with the gun.

Cassidy, after a while, drew the buggy to a halt. Casting a glance over her shoulder, saw Josh being hustled away at gunpoint by the rough-looking man. Determination set in her jaw, and she resolutely turned her gaze back to the road, steering the buggy back toward

Duloe. As the nearest stand of scrubby trees came into view, she spotted Grey on his horse, waiting for her in the shadows.

"I saw everything," he called out as she approached. "Josh is still a captive, but the boy is free. And one man lies dead. "

Cassidy looked back, her face solemn as she saw Josh being bundled away.

Grey remained on his horse, his eyes fixed on the empty scene behind them, save for the still figure lying on the ground. "There was nothing more you could have done, Cassidy. Getting away with the little one was the best choice."

Charlie had climbed up to sit beside Cassidy, and snuggled under her arm.

Cassidy put an arm around Charlie. "Don't worry, we'll get your father another time." Her voice was calm and betrayed none of that inner turmoil she felt at the sight of Josh being held captive by such a violent, unscrupulous man.

The small boy looked up at her, and she smiled down at him. He gave her an odd little smile in return. "Thank you," he said politely. As Cassidy told Grey later, it was almost as if she was giving him a biscuit. He was far too quiet after the stressful time he had endured.

"Grey, where should I take him?" Cassidy asked, her voice low but urgent. "I'm almost certain I saw R-U-T-H"—she spelled the name out carefully, mindful that Charlie was listening. "I think she was hiding from me in the boarding house. She must have been in on the kidnap attempt plot. They could not have done it without her."

Grey's brows furrowed in concern. His horse became restless, as if sensing the disquiet in the man on his back.

"You think Charlie's in danger if you take him back there? Surely not …" He sat motionless for a moment, lost in thought as he weighed the options Cassidy faced.

Charlie, seated beside her, looked up at her with wide, frightened eyes. She tightened her arm around him and whispered, "Don't worry, we'll get your father back another time. But for now, we need to find a safe place for you and get you a nice meal." The little boy nodded solemnly, his face etched with a seriousness beyond his years.

"He's too quiet," Grey observed softly, his eyes lingering on the boy. "He's been through too much lately."

Suddenly, the sound of hoofbeats broke the silence, and they turned to see Sam riding up to them. "No good, Cassidy—there was nothing we could do to save Josh," he called out to her.

Sam greeted them, his face set in angry lines. "Hello, Grey. My men and I couldn't do anything. Any sudden move could have turned disastrous. The man holding Josh was dead set on causing trouble. Too unpredictable to take a chance on Josh's life."

"Yes, Sam, I didn't like the look of him either," Cassidy replied. "He seemed unstable, ready to snap at any moment. You did well to keep your distance. We're just trying to decide where to take Charlie. Whether to risk going back to Duloe, or …"

As her voice trailed off, Sam's gaze fell on the little boy, who stared back at him in wide-eyed amazement. "You're an Indian," Charlie said with a child-like bluntness, his English accent thick and clear, drawing a smile from the adults.

Sam chuckled softly. "That I am, little one." Then,

turning serious, he addressed Cassidy again. "What if I take him? He could join the other children at Dry Creek Ranch. There are other kids there now, and Amy would keep him safe in good company. My men could watch over the ranch."

Grey nodded in agreement. "That makes sense, Cassidy. You need to be close to Duloe in case there's another ransom demand for Josh. But Charlie would be safer away from there, among friends."

Cassidy looked down at the boy beside her. "Charlie, this is my good friend, Sam. He's part Indian. Would you like to go for a ride with him?"

Charlie glanced between Cassidy and Sam, then nodded, his trust clear in his solemn gaze. "All right," he whispered, his voice small but steady.

Cassidy smiled, brushing a strand of hair away from his face. "That's a brave boy," she whispered, her heart aching for the child who had already endured so much. "You'll be safe with Sam, I promise."

"Will you ride on my horse with me?" Sam said, and rode nearer to the buggy.

"You'll be quite safe with Sam," Cassidy repeated and helped the little boy reach over to be lifted into Sam's arms.

"Okay, little fella?" Sam said, settling the small boy in front of him.

Charlie looked at Cassidy for reassurance. At her smile of encouragement, he gave her tentative smile back and, with a wave from Sam, he was gone into the darkness of the night.

CHAPTER THIRTY-SEVEN

Grey and Cassidy made their way back toward the boarding house. They had left their horses and Cassidy's buggy at the livery stables. Night was almost upon them now. Lanterns swung outside the saloons and those stores that stayed open late at night in the hopes of further customers. The decline in the miners' custom made them all eager for further trade. At first, the two walked along in silence. The botched kidnap ransom drop was uppermost in their thoughts. Figures passed them by, unseen by them.

As they walked, Cassidy's mind raced. She had to return now and face the two women in the boarding house. Both, she felt, were involved in the kidnap of Josh and Charlie. "I need to figure out what to say when I get there. What will I tell them? Where have I been?" she muttered, more to herself than Grey.

"Tell them you were talking to your lawyer," Grey suggested, his brow furrowed as he tried to work things out in his mind. The relief he had felt on Cassidy escaping unscathed from the botched ransom handover had left him in a quandary. Grey was amazed at how vitally important her safety and security meant to him. Walking along beside her, his thoughts were muddled. The petite figure strolling along beside him was completely unaware that her beauty, even in the shadowy main street of Duloe, was attracting attention from men passing by. Her beauty had first caught his attention, but it was her courage and loyalty to her friends that had brought about his deep affection for her. Better think about those thoughts and work out what he was going to do about them later. Not now. "Your lawyer couldn't see you during the day and you have to go back to Nowhere tomorrow. So he spoke to you this evening."

"Do you think they will believe that? Sounds a flimsy excuse to me." Cassidy replied.

"Doesn't matter if they believe it or not, just give it as your reason for going out."

They were approaching the boarding house now, and Cassidy felt an unease sweep over her as she rehearsed the words she was going to say to the boarding house landlady in her mind.

Grey grabbed her arm. "It's Sam! Look, he's riding toward us. What is he doing back here, and he's on his own?"

Surprised that Sam should be back already in Duloe, Cassidy asked, worry apparent in her voice, "Charlie? Sam! What's happened to Charlie? "

Sam replied, slowing to a stop. "Charlie's fine. He's with my young cousin. I've never seen Charlie laugh like that before. My cousin's got a way of making everyone laugh. They've taken Charlie and gone on ahead. Don't worry. I figured I'd be more useful here, Cassidy."

Sam jumped off his horse, and, leading it beside them, he continued speaking.

"They will see him safe to the ranch. Meanwhile, I've come back with a couple of others to help sort this mess out. That man who's holding Josh? We know him. Killed a couple of our tribe long ago, took everything they had for no reason but sport. We have a score to settle with that man!"

Both Cassidy and Grey stared at Sam, speechless. Finally, Grey spoke up. "If that's what brought you back here, Sam, I'm just glad you're with us."

Cassidy took a deep breath. Grey leaned down toward

her. "Just remember, Charlie is safe. That's the most important thing."

CHAPTER THIRTY-EIGHT

Cassidy gave him a weak smile and walked across the boardwalk to the boarding house. She pushed open the door with a practiced calm, hiding her inner turmoil. Immediately, she heard someone scrambling into another room from the hall. The back of the fleeing figure was familiar. Cassidy almost called out to Ruth but decided against it. Patience, she reminded herself.

Lil appeared, her large frame looming over Cassidy as she hurried to meet her. Cassidy gave her a sweet smile and said, "Goodnight, Lil." She edged past Lil and raced up the stairs, not giving the other woman a chance to speak. Once inside her room, Cassidy took off her hat and coat, throwing them on the bed. She placed one gun on the nightstand. Cassidy stood by the window, staring out into the inky blackness of the night. Her mind swirled with thoughts about the other women in the boarding house. Who could be trusted in this place? What was their next move? She didn't have long to wait.

A knock at the door startled her. Her hand instinctively went for the gun, which she held behind her back as she approached the door cautiously. "Who is it?"

"It's just me—Lil," came the reply. "I brought you some tea and supper. I thought you might welcome something to eat and drink."

Cassidy unlocked the door and opened it, watching as Lil entered the room with a tray. The woman wore a smile. It was too sweet, too forced, for Cassidy's liking. Lil placed the tray on the dressing table: a pot of tea, a cup and saucer, and a plate of cold meats and bread. Lil's smile was looking out of place in the tense atmosphere. Never had Lil given her any attention like this before.

Cassidy said her thanks and went toward the dressing table, but her eyes never left Lil. The game was afoot, and Cassidy was determined to stay one step ahead. The woman smiled at her as she left the room, but Cassidy knew the danger from the large woman hadn't passed. She would have to tread carefully in the coming hours. The long night ahead was far from over, and Cassidy wasn't sure who her true allies were.

She poured herself a cup of tea and sat down by the window again, her mind working through the tangled web she found herself in.

Shouts came from Main Street at the entrance to Duloe Town. Cassidy jumped up and went to the window. The noise grew louder and closer the further it came down the street, toward the boarding house. She watched from her window as the grim procession passed below, a crowd of onlookers trailing behind, eager to discover what had happened.

Cassidy stared down at the man draped lifelessly over his horse as he was led into the town. The eager crowd following the dead body knew the sheriff would soon be asking questions, and each of them wanted to be there to hear the details firsthand. As Cassidy watched, the door to the building below her opened, and Lil and Ruth rushed out to look at the body of the dead man.

Cassidy retreated slightly behind the curtain, watching as the women hurried toward the body. One of them, on seeing the dead man, cried out to the man leading the horse, "Stop! It's him, he's dead!" Her voice rose in a shriek, then dissolved into a wail of anguish. "She killed him! If she didn't, she must know what happened!"

The two women turned toward the window, and

Cassidy was glad that she was hidden behind the curtain. Cassidy recognized Ruth by the light of the oil lamp she was carrying. That was the same Ruth who had once been so kind to little Charlie, and who had promised to care for him and return him to his home in England. Somehow, Ruth's betrayal of that small boy felt far worse to Cassidy than any treachery toward an adult like Josh. How could Ruth, who had cradled Charlie as if he were her own, hand him over to the clutches of evil kidnappers?

Cassidy's mind was full of her thoughts of Ruth while she prepared herself for Ruth's inevitable arrival at her bedroom door. In the few minutes she knew had, she swiftly packed the few belongings she had brought with her. Sliding a pistol beneath the folds of the bedcover beside her, she sat on the bed, braced for Ruth's entrance. It didn't take long. Her bedroom door was soon unlocked. The landlady obviously had another key. As the door swung open, it revealed Ruth in the doorway. Gone was her warm, pleasant expression, her face now a mask of anger and grief.

"What happened? What did you do? Who killed him? Did *you* kill him?" Ruth demanded, her voice sharp. She strode into the room and glared down at Cassidy, her fist clenching and unclenching as if she would strike the young woman sitting on the bed.

Cassidy closed the small book she had on her lap, glancing up as if startled by the intrusion. She put on a look of bewilderment. "Why, Ruth? What are you doing here? I thought you were on your way to England."

"You know exactly why I'm here. Where's the letter you received this afternoon? What did you do after you read it?" Ruth snapped.

Cassidy maintained her puzzled expression and

pointed to the dresser. "That silly note? It's crumpled up over there." Ruth's gaze followed her finger, and, sure enough, the note lay discarded. "A ridiculous message about gold and a lonely spot," Cassidy added with a laugh. "As if I'd go off alone to some unknown place. What could they possibly want with me?"

Holding her composure, Cassidy studied the irate woman standing before her. She could see Ruth hesitate, momentarily unsure, but then the woman regained her resolve.

"Where were you?" Ruth demanded, hands on her hips. "You haven't been in your room all night."

"I was up at the Chinese restaurant and then I met with my lawyer," Cassidy replied smoothly. "My friend's thinking of buying it from the owner, who's planning to leave Duloe and head for the new gold fields out West. My lawyer is dealing with the legal stuff. Go on and ask him if you don't believe me."

Ruth's hands remained on her hips, her face twisted with doubt and suspicion. Nearby, Lil had been watching the exchange closely, and now she spoke up. "So, if you know nothing about a letter concerning two packages, why did you come to Duloe? Why are you even here if not to retrieve whatever it is you've lost?"

Her meaning was clear to Cassidy, but she ignored it. She would not fall into that trap. Cassidy's face darkened as she stood up, glaring at both women. "I have business with the lawyer here," she retorted, "and I'm helping my friend with the restaurant. What do you mean by this intrusion, anyway? Why have you burst in here, demanding answers and making accusations?" She shook her head, disgusted. "If this is how you treat guests, I don't think I'll be staying any longer. I'm going to the hotel."

With a snap, Cassidy closed her book, slipping it into her bag. Her gun she slid into her skirt pocket, then reached for her coat draped over the bed. Before Ruth or Lil could react, she strode out of the room.

As she descended the stairs, Cassidy kept one hand on her pistol and the other tightly gripping her bag. Every step she felt weighted down by the prickling sense that Ruth and Lil might follow her, perhaps even attempt to shoot her. But her calm responses and resolute attitude seemed to have left the women uncertain and off-balance, buying her enough time to slip away.

Without hesitation, Cassidy headed for the livery stables. If luck was on her side, Tom might be there, or even Grey, awaiting the morning's light before heading back to Nowhere. Not an ideal resting place for the night, she thought, but she'd slept in far worse places. At least it might be safer in the stable rather than under the same roof as Ruth and Lil.

The night was dark, but as the clouds shifted the narrow street leading to the stables was illuminated in a silvery glow, bright as day. Cassidy's mind raced. If they were there, perhaps they could hire a horse and resume their journey before Ruth and Lil could regroup. Cassidy had to get back to Nowhere, the sooner the better. Duloe was not a safe place for her any longer.

CHAPTER THIRTY-NINE

Hurrying toward the livery stable, Cassidy kept looking behind her. She told them she was going to the hotel. If they came after her, they would look there first. She must reach the livery stable and be out of sight before they came out of the boarding house.

Light streamed out of the livery stable through the half-open door. Approaching with caution, Cassidy stood behind the door, listening. The voices reassured Cassidy. She recognized Sam's quiet speech and Lance Grey's measured tones. Pushing open the door, she entered, feeling a wave of relief at the sight of the two men seated beside the fire burning in a brazier at the front of the stable.

"Cassidy? Are you all right?" Grey sprang to his feet as soon as he saw her, rushing to take her bag and help her settle onto a stool beside the fire. "We thought you would stay the night at the boarding house."

"So did I," she replied, her voice tinged with frustration. "But the sight of the dead man being taken to the sheriff's office sent Ruth into a vicious temper. She turned on me, accusing me of killing her man. I told her I had gone to the Chinese restaurant and talked to my lawyer and ignored the note. But she didn't believe me. Luckily, I had already packed and was getting ready to leave when they barged into my bedroom."

"Did they hurt you, Cassidy?" Sam asked, his concern clear. He had also risen to his feet, and now his deep brown eyes searched her face intently.

Grey, who had gone to pour coffee for her, turned sharply to stare at Cassidy as well, awaiting her response.

Cassidy shook her head. "No, I'm fine. I pushed past

them and ran out of the hotel. I thought they might follow me, but I don't think they bothered."

Handing her a steaming mug of coffee, Grey looked down at her, his gaze scrutinising her appearance for any signs of harm. Meanwhile, Sam moved to the door, which Cassidy had shut firmly behind her. He cracked it open, peering out onto the main street of Duloe Town. After a brief glance, he closed it again and placed the wooden bar across it to secure the doorway. Then he returned to join them by the fire.

"Could you travel tonight, Cassidy?" he asked, his voice steady but urgent.

Cassidy drained the last dregs of her coffee and set the mug down. "Of course I can travel tonight. I was hoping we could do that. I'd like to get out of Duloe Town. Josh will have been taken far away from here. Do you intend to ride, or shall we take a buggy? I prefer to ride. It's quicker. "

Sam nodded to Grey. "I'll get the horses ready. I suggest we head toward Dry Creek Ranch. They'll expect Cassidy to go straight to Nowhere. This way, we might shake them off if they're following her."

It didn't take long to prepare. The fire in the brazier was doused, and Cassidy followed the men down the row of horses. Grey's sleek black horse greeted him with a soft nicker. Sam saddled up a pretty young mare that nodded her head at Cassidy in welcome. Taking her bag, Sam strapped it onto the horse's back, but as he prepared to lead the animal out, Cassidy reached for the reins.

"I've got her. You get your own horse, Sam."

Lance Grey was already at the stable door, half of it open. His own horse stood ready behind him. He took his time, checking to ensure the coast was clear. Satisfied, he opened the door fully, allowing Cassidy and Sam to exit first. Pulling the door shut behind him, he mounted his horse, and the three of them began to ride out of town.

Before they could disappear into the night, a shout rang out behind them. Cassidy glanced back and saw Ruth and her landlady friend running down the main street. Though they had spotted the trio, it was unlikely they could mount up and follow quickly enough to catch them. They were soon out of range and out of the town itself.

The moonlight, though obscured by intermittent clouds, illuminated the way ahead well enough. Lance Grey led the way, his long black coat-tails flying behind him as he rode at a steady pace. Cassidy followed closely, conscious of Sam bringing up the rear. For the first time that night, she felt a sense of safety.

Maintaining her composure at the hotel had been an exhausting ordeal. Ruth's animosity toward her had been palpable and unnerving, though Cassidy couldn't fathom its source. Ruth had been the one to betray the gentle little boy, handing him over to the kidnappers. She had smilingly accepted the money from Josh, assuring him of her care and affection for the child. Yet Ruth seemed to feel justified in her actions, her rage directed at Cassidy instead of feeling guilt herself.

Why should Ruth feel aggrieved? Cassidy wondered. Why should Ruth's betrayal of Josh and little Charlie leave her feeling self-righteous?

Cassidy shook her head, dismissing the thought. That puzzle remained unsolved. Other matters demanded her attention. More urgent was the need to shake off any pursuers and to uncover Josh's whereabouts. Still in the hands of the kidnappers, his life remained in peril. Would they demand another ransom, or had they more sinister intentions?

These were the questions that filled Cassidy's mind as they rode into the night. Determined to stay one step ahead of danger, her security, and safety were not only her concern but that of her companions, Sam, and Grey. They rode into the night feeling with each mile more relaxed and more certain of their safety.

Shaking her head, Cassidy pushed the troubling questions aside. There were more pressing matters. They had to evade Ruth and her gang, and, more importantly, they needed to track down Josh. His life was still in danger!

CHAPTER FORTY

The journey around the foothills of Devil's Mountain from Duloe Town to Dry Creek Ranch was not that long, but it had become bitterly cold. The mild autumn air had been replaced by a biting wind, and Cassidy shivered. Winter had held off while they had a mild autumn. But it went into winter today. Cassidy noticed Sam riding up beside her. Without a word, he retrieved a blanket from his saddlebag and handed it to her.

"Thank you, Sam," she murmured gratefully, wrapping it tightly around herself. The mare beneath her tolerated the movement as she adjusted herself in the blanket, and the added warmth was a welcome relief. Cassidy resolved to toast herself by the fire at Dry Creek Ranch and change into something more suitable for the even colder weather that was on its way.

A day of unexpected drama and frightening emotions had filled Cassidy's day. The repetitive movements of the horse as it plodded along lulled Cassidy into a sleepy state. Or it would have done if she hadn't been so cold. The familiar ranch fence brought relief; she was almost there.

Lance Grey called out to warn the homestead of their arrival. A welcoming shout greeted them, and the warm light spilling from the open door was a beacon of comfort. Two members of Sam's group, rifles in hand, stood ready alongside Tom and Amy. Those at Dry Creek Ranch had not been left unprotected. Tom stepped forward to grab the reins of one horse while the others led the animals to the stable.

Cassidy, instead of jumping off her horse in a usual manner, slid off her horse to land tangled up with the blanket.

"Cassidy! What are you doing here, Cassidy? What brings you to Dry Creek Ranch?" Amy exclaimed, rushing forward to guide Cassidy inside. Once through the door, Cassidy almost ran to the stove, stretching her hands out toward the welcoming heat.

"I got so cold," she murmured with a faint smile. Her teeth were chattering, and her hands were blue with the cold. "That wind! It's growing colder by the day. I thought it best to dress well for a meeting with the lawyer and banker. I rushed out of the boarding house, still wearing my costume. It was not the right choice for a ride to Dry Creek Ranch! I'll need something warmer now that I'm no longer in Duloe Town."

Her grateful hands were cupped around the hot coffee, and still Cassidy stood shivering beside the stove.

"You can borrow some of my clothes," Amy offered hesitantly. "They're not as fine as yours, though. But they will keep you warm." Amy knew Cassidy always dressed in the finest quality garments when she was in town and felt embarrassed by the few garments she had in her own cupboard.

"I'll gladly take anything you can spare," Cassidy replied earnestly. "We left in such a hurry, and I packed only a little when I set out."

The small ranch house was soon bustling with activity. Satisfied that Charlie was now sleeping peacefully after his traumatic experiences of the day, Cassidy could relax. The room was crowded as everyone sought warmth and comfort. The tiny Chinese girl was asleep in Amy's bedroom, exhausted after the flight from the cafe. Tom's face was grim as he seated himself at the table, while the two men from Sam's group murmured quietly with him.

Grey sipped thoughtfully at his coffee, and Amy busied herself offering food, though no one seemed hungry, only thirsty and tired.

"What's our next move?" Cassidy asked as she finally joined them at the table.

Grey set his cup down and considered the question. "We sleep. A few hours of rest, and then we follow their tracks. I don't think it's worth going to Nowhere to gather more men. Do you, Sam?"

Sam shook his head. "No. With my group and yourself, that should be enough. I have two more men who will join us. They lost family to these villains." His words, whispered, carried a chilling weight.

"And don't forget me," Cassidy said firmly.

Amy sighed in frustration. "I wish I could come too."

"You need to stay and protect Charlie and the others," Cassidy gently reminded her.

After the plans were made, space cleared, and blankets found, each person curled up and caught a few hours of sleep before morning arrived. The plans they had laid out the night before felt solid, practical, and would give the best outcome. That was until they woke up!

CHAPTER FORTY-ONE

Snow! The entire landscape had been transformed overnight. Their plans were useless now. All the time spent working them out and thinking them through had been a waste of time. Snow had blanketed all the tracks they intended to follow. The kidnappers could have gone in any direction, and the snowfall had obliterated every sign of their passing.

"I'm heading into Nowhere," Lance Grey muttered grimly, staring into his cup of coffee. His voice carried a note of resignation. "There's no need to rush now. Tracking them will take time, and it'll be far more difficult." He drained the last of his coffee and set the cup down on the table with a heavy thud. Looking around at the roomful of people slowly waking up, he asked, "Anyone else want to head into Nowhere with me?"

"I'll come," Cassidy replied without hesitation, her words clipped but resolute. "I think they might send another ransom note, and they'll expect me to stay close by waiting for news from the kidnappers. I'll wait for some contact from them at the hotel." Cassidy reached for her cup, sipping the coffee, her mind already thinking about the next steps she should take.

Amy came out from the bedroom and gestured toward a cupboard against the bedroom wall. "Cassidy, come and look at these jackets." She opened the cupboard and stepped back to let Cassidy see its contents. "These were Nancy's. She left them here. They're what she always wore when she lived here at the ranch. The ones on the other side are mine."

Cassidy moved closer, peering into the cupboard. The collection of jackets spoke volumes about their owner.

She felt Amy's discomfort, sensing her unease in revealing how few garments she owned. But Cassidy herself was no stranger to frugality. She remembered a time when her own wardrobe had been far more threadbare than Amy's modest collection.

"This one," Cassidy said after a moment. Her eyes had lit up at the sight of a large sheepskin coat hanging at the far end of the rail. Reaching out, she touched it and then pulled it toward her. "I'll take this one." Cassidy lifted it off the peg. It was heavy and very thick. She lifted it up and gave a laugh. "This is perfect. It should keep me warm."

The coat dwarfed her as she shrugged into it. Nancy had been a tall, broad woman, while Cassidy was petite and slight. The heavy coat enveloped her completely. Her arms were hidden from view, only the tips of her fingers protruding from the sleeves.

"Are you sure, Cassidy? It's enormous on you," Amy said, the concern clear in her voice. Amy stared at the petite Cassidy, dwarfed by the voluminous sheepskin coat.

"I'll be warm, if not hot, in this coat," Cassidy replied. "It was so cold with a bitter wind, traveling here last night. I don't care how it looks. On my next journey, I just want to be warm." She paused and regarded Amy. "Do you need it, though? I don't want to take something you'll use."

Amy shook her head, a small laugh escaping her lips. The freckles on her face joined up across the cheeks as she giggled at the very idea of wearing the coat herself. "Goodness, no. It's way too big for me. I'd never be able to move around in it."

Before Amy could say more, a loud wail erupted from

the other room. She shot Cassidy an apologetic glance before rushing out to tend to young David, her footsteps echoing in the quiet house.

Voices came from the other small bedroom—young, childish voices. Cassidy remembered that young David's cousin Flora was living there. As she listened to the cheerful chatter, she could hear the clipped English tones of Charlie. To Cassidy's relief, the boy was joining in the conversation, and she even heard him laugh. It had been worth yesterday's ransom fiasco just to hear Charlie's laughter this morning.

Cassidy stood there for a moment, watching her friend disappear down the hall, then turned her gaze to the coat. She ran her hands along its thick, comforting pile. She shrugged herself into it and pulled it tighter around her shoulders. If nothing else, the coat promised a wonderful layer of protection in the uncertain hours ahead. Standing on tiptoe, Cassidy peered into the chipped and broken piece of mirror standing on a shelf. She smiled at her reflection, which was no longer smart or stylish. Her face peered out from behind the sheepskin collar. Wonderful, Cassidy thought—this would be perfect for the snow and blizzards she was about to ride into.

The snow had made everyone think again. All their plans were in disarray. There would be no chasing after the kidnappers this morning. The tracks would be covered in thick snow in no time. So Cassidy and Grey set off into the growing blizzard, determined to track them down later. First, they were going to head into Nowhere. Grey would attend to the sheriff's duties and gather two or three men that would join him tracking down the kidnappers when the weather had cleared.

Sam, along with his two Indian brothers, were going

to attempt to find the tracks, despite the worsening weather. They were determined to catch the men who had killed their family members for sport.

"We shall set off, despite the falling snow. Perhaps we will get lucky and find a trace of them, and work out where they are heading," Sam said, gazing out the window at the snow, which was falling steadily again. The tracks left by Grey and Cassidy were already disappearing under a fine, powdery layer.

"You're going to look for my father?" The boy's polite English accent made everyone stop what they were doing to listen. Sam smiled down at the small boy standing beside him. Charlie had hardly spoken since his arrival. Though he had smiled politely at cheerful comments and accepted the food and drink given to him,

Amy had noted with growing concern how quiet Charlie was. Now, for the first time, he volunteered a remark. Amy watched, waiting to see what would happen next. The small boy, when she first saw him, had been dressed in a suit, with collar and tie. The blond hair, so like his father's, had been smoothed back into order. For all the world dressed like a little gentleman, he had been reserved, fearful of speaking out of turn. Amy wondered what sort of life he had led in England. From what she heard from the manservant that Josh's older brother had brought with him from England, it had been a life of rigid formality. Now his suit was ripped in places, his hair flopping down just like his father's. But still the boy seemed closed in on himself. That remark had been the first he had made.

"Yes, the three of us will go and see if we can find where the bad men have taken him," Sam replied. "We'll meet up with Grey and a few other men, and then we'll find him and get him away to safety." The boy's solemn face gave nothing away, but he nodded.

"What happens if you don't find him?" Charlie's apprehensive eyes turned to Amy, then Tom, and finally up to the Indian man standing beside him. "What happens then?"

CHAPTER FORTY-TWO

Amy stepped forward. She crouched down to Charlie's level and placed a comforting arm around him. "Charlie, you don't have to worry. If we don't find your father, I'm certain your uncle will want you back in England. Until then, you'll be safe here with us. But Charlie, I don't think you have to worry at all. Sam, Grey and Cassidy always get the men they're searching for." Amy embraced the boy, but he stiffened in her arms, managing only a faint smile. Amy felt at a loss. She didn't know how to reach the boy.

Flora joined her, grasping Charlie's hand. "Come on, Charlie. You've got to help me with David. He wants to play in the snow, but it's too cold right now. Let's keep him busy and give Amy a break."

Charlie looked at Flora, gave her his solemn nod and, taking her hand, walked off with Flora to join David.

Meanwhile, Tom was chatting with the small Chinese girl, in her own language, who sat silently watching the comings and goings in the ranch house.

Sam came up behind Amy and whispered in her ear, "You've got your hands full. First, you take my nephew into your home. And young David, he's a real handful. And now you have Charlie. Hopefully, only for a short time until his father is found, and now a Chinese girl. Josh always told me you collect stray people like others collect stray dogs." His eyes were warm and teasing as they lingered on her.

Amy felt her cheeks grow warm under his gaze. She tried to fight the blush rising in her neck and face, but it was more than just his remarks that unsettled her. It was the way his eyes softened when they looked at her, holding something deeper within them than friendship.

For so long, Amy had thought she was in love with Josh. But, over time, she realized that what she felt for him was closer to the fondness one feels for a brother. The thought of opening her heart to someone else, someone like Sam, was both exhilarating and terrifying.

The sky hung low and grey that afternoon, casting a heavy stillness over the land stretching beyond Dry Creek Ranch. Later in the morning, the two boys from the Hobbs's Ranch had arrived, shaking snow from their hair and boots. Their sudden entrance had brought a flurry of laughter.

"Our father got sick of us hanging around the house, especially now the snow's here. Miss Amy, he said you wanted us to work for you, so here we are!" they had announced cheerfully.

Amy vaguely remembered discussing this arrangement in passing with Mr. Hobbs last month, but no dates had been confirmed. Nor had they talked about wages or accommodation. Yet, here the two young lads were, and with the snow coming down even heavier there was no way she could send them back.

"I'm surprised to see you," she said. "Your father didn't tell me when you were coming. But you're both welcome, especially since we may face some trouble soon."

Tom took charge of the young men, leading them out to the barn where they would sleep and live until another room could be built. With their help, Amy planned to fix up another outbuilding to give them more permanent accommodation.

Later, when they returned to the house, Amy asked what arrangements their father had made for payment.

"What has he told you, because he arranged nothing with me?" Amy said, quite annoyed at the sudden arrival of both boys.

"We work for you, you feed us and maybe give us a little money when times are good," the older boy said with a grin. "Our father has too many mouths to feed. Thought you could do with our help and feed us into the bargain."

They had all soon settled into life at the ranch that day, much to Amy's relief. Despite the cramped quarters, the ranch now felt more secure with the two young men's presence. Especially if Ruth made another attempt to take Charlie. That thought alone made Amy silently grateful for their arrival.

Later that evening, as the snow continued to fall outside, she felt an odd mix of weariness and hopefulness. Life at the ranch was unpredictable, but she thought that with the people around her, she could face whatever challenges lay ahead. But could she?

CHAPTER FORTY-THREE

Grey and Cassidy rode side by side, their heads bent low against the driving snow. A bitter wind howled down from the peaks of Devil's Mountain, leaving no chance for conversation. Any sound was swallowed by the storm, making speech impossible as their horses trudged toward Nowhere.

Grey had pulled his heavy black coat tightly around his body, his shoulders hunched to brace against the relentless cold. The coat collar was turned up as high as it could go, and his hat was rammed down onto his head, shielding his face from the icy blasts.

Cassidy, more prepared than she had been at the start of their journey from Duloe, wore the huge sheepskin jacket she had borrowed from Amy's cupboard. The coat that had once belonged to Nancy and was so large it nearly reached her ankles. Before departing, she and Amy had shared a laugh as they cinched a belt around her waist to keep the oversized garment in place. Now, seated on her horse, the furry collar of the coat was pulled snugly up to her ears, and a woolen shawl was wrapped around her head. For the first time, Cassidy felt warm and snug, even if she no longer looked smart or elegant. Keeping warm was more important than looking stylish!

The journey to Dry Creek Ranch from Duloe began with Cassidy inadequately dressed for the harsh weather. But now, well-insulated against the elements—thanks to the coat—she focused only on their destination and what she was going to do when she reached Nowhere. Approaching the small township, they could see the faint outlines of the settlement ahead, the buildings of Nowhere flickering into view through the flurries of snow before vanishing again in the storm's fury.

"I didn't think we'd make it," Grey muttered through near-frozen lips as he drew closer to Cassidy. His voice was hoarse and strained, the words almost lost to the wind. As they reached the outskirts of town, he continued, "Wait for me at the hotel. I'll settle things with my deputy, see if I can round up a couple of men, and then we'll head off to meet the others."

"Do you think we can travel in this weather?" Cassidy shouted, her voice nearly carried away by the howling wind. "We have to be careful not to get stranded. It could mean certain death."

Grey edged his horse nearer to hers. "We'll give it a few hours and see," he said. "If the storm eases, we can make for the cave where Reuben stayed. From there, we'll get a clearer view of how bad things are up on Devil's Mountain before we decide to continue."

Cassidy nodded, leaning closer to him so her words wouldn't be lost. "Let me know when you're ready to leave. I'll decide then whether to go with you or stay behind in case the kidnapper contacts me."

Their conversation ended as the urgency of the storm pressed them onward and Main Street itself was coming into view. Together, they urged their weary horses into Nowhere; they, too, were eager to find shelter from the relentless wind and snow.

At the livery stable, Grey dismounted first, fighting against the gusts to hold the door open for Cassidy and her horse. She led her mount inside, turning back to take Grey's reins while he wrestled to close the door behind them. With both horses safely inside, Cassidy watched as the old stableman shuffled over, shaking his head at the weather.

"Lucky you made it," the old man grumbled, his voice gruff. "Not many survive a blizzard like this. Terrible weather." He shook his head again as he took the reins from Cassidy and led the horses deeper into the stable. "Terrible weather. Terrible," he repeated, taking the horses.

Grey brushed the snow from his shoulders, his coat shedding snowballs as he joined Cassidy. "I'll walk you to the hotel," he said, pulling the stable door open against the force of the wind. "Can't have you blown away."

Normally proud of her independence, Cassidy found herself grateful for Grey's steadying arm as they made their way down the empty, snow-covered street. The wind buffeted her from all sides, shrieking like a living thing. At the hotel door, they paused under the small shelter of the porch.

Grey pushed the door open and gestured for Cassidy to go inside. Leaning close, he whispered, "Take care. I'll be in my office if you need me. Watch your back."

CHAPTER FORTY-FOUR

Cassidy nodded as he stepped away, the wind and snow swallowing his retreating footsteps. Feeling a sudden pang of loneliness, she shoved the thought aside and focused on warming herself. Inside, she stamped her feet on the mat, shaking off clumps of snow that clung to her boots and coat.

Dora, the owner, rushed down the hall to greet her. Her finger was at her lips. "Hush! say nothing. Keep quiet!" She seized Cassidy by the arm and pushed her into the small, dimly lit room that served as her office. "Ruth was here earlier. She was looking for you," Dora said, her tone urgent. "She thought you'd be here already. Where have you been? How did you manage to get here through this blizzard? "

Cassidy, surprised at finding Ruth already at the hotel, paused in the act of unfastening her enormous coat. Her eyes widened in surprise. "How did she get here so quickly?" she asked, her voice tinged with disbelief. "I didn't expect the wagon to make it through from Duloe in this weather."

"She didn't use the wagon," Dora replied, stepping closer to help Cassidy remove the heavy coat. "Ruth rode all the way here with another woman and a rough-looking man. A man who gave me a very bad feeling. I don't trust any of them, but there's something evil about that man. He frightened me."

Dora draped the coat over a chair, smoothing the sheepskin with an absent-minded stroke. She glanced up at Cassidy, curiosity plain in her expression. "By the way, where did you get this coat? It doesn't seem like something you'd usually wear."

Cassidy chuckled, the soft sound tinged with a weariness that only long journeys and colder weather could inspire. "It's Nancy's. Amy found it in a cupboard over at Dry Creek Ranch and gave it to me. I was frozen stiff after the trip from Duloe to Dry Creek Ranch. This coat saved me. It kept me warm the entire way here."

"I'm not surprised," Dora said with a smile, running her hand over the heavy jacket. "It's big enough to keep both of us warm." She moved to a nearby shelf, retrieving a bottle of whiskey and two glasses. Pouring a generous measure into each, she handed one to Cassidy. "This will warm you up even more."

Cassidy accepted the glass gratefully, taking a sip of the amber liquid as Dora settled into a chair. Cassidy held the glass in both hands and snuggled back deep into the chair beside the stove. The warmth was so welcome, and she could feel her muscles relaxing for the first time since she left Dry Creek Ranch. In between sips of the whiskey, Cassidy told Dora of the ransom drop at the lightning tree.

"At least Charlie is safe with Amy at Dry Creek Ranch. But now Josh is still a captive," Dora gazed into her own glass, swirling the whiskey, the light of the oil lamp refracting through the warm hues. "What are you going to do, Cassidy?" she asked quietly. "What now?"

Cassidy rose from the chair and started pacing the small space between the furniture of Dora's office. Then she stopped pacing. The tiny figure of Cassidy perched on the edge of the large desk, her brow furrowed as she stared at the floor, deep in thought. Her mind was a whirlwind of conflicting ideas and unanswered questions. Was it the oppressive cold clouding her judgment, or was it the sheer weight of the problems bearing down on her?

She couldn't find a clear path forward. What should be her next action?

One thing was certain: Josh had to be her priority. Everything else paled in comparison. But how to proceed? Bargaining with Ruth was an option, but it came with its own risks. Their previous encounter at the lightning tree had left Cassidy painfully aware of how untrustworthy the kidnapper could be. He had shot and killed his own partner. Yet if she didn't deal with Ruth, how would she maintain any connection to the kidnappers? The uncertainty gnawed at her.

"I'm struggling, Dora. Do I wait for a ransom note? Grey is going to join Sam to search out the kidnappers. Do I go with them or wait here?"

Both women sat silent as they tried to think of a way forward.

"Ruth seemed anxious," Dora murmured, breaking the silence. "I don't think she knows what's going on with Josh. Her contact with the kidnappers had to have been that dead man. Without him, I'm betting she's just as clueless as we are."

Cassidy nodded, the wheels in her mind turning. "That makes sense. If Ruth doesn't know what's happening, then she's probably come here hoping to gather information. She wants to ensure she gets her share of the ransom money." She sighed, rubbing her temples. "The question is, how do I use that to our advantage?"

Dora leaned forward, her voice steady. "We'll figure it out. But you need to stay sharp, Cassidy. Whatever Ruth's motivations, she's dangerous. We can't afford to trust her."

The room fell into a heavy silence, the weight of the situation pressing down on both women. Outside, the wind howled, rattling the windows as if nature itself were warning them of further storms that lay ahead.

CHAPTER FORTY-FIVE

Both women sat in the deepening silence, sipping their whiskey, their thoughts consumed by the mounting problems they faced. Only the movement of a log crumbling into flames in the stove in front of them made a sound. Each woman was thinking of Josh and his predicament. Josh had unexpectedly entered their lives, his cheerful good humor and helpful manners, combined with his peculiar English accent, endearing him to both of them. Now, he was in grave danger, and they were determined to do everything within their power to secure his release from the kidnappers.

Relief had washed over Josh's friends when his son, Charlie, was rescued. The man who had taken him was cruel, his malevolence clear when he killed his companion without a second thought when they argued about the gold. Knowing Josh was at the mercy of such a villain was too dreadful to dwell upon. They sat on, the whiskey in their glasses had been drunk. But still both women sat, trying to think of the way ahead.

The silence in the room was abruptly interrupted by the sound of footsteps and muffled voices in the hall. Dora's instincts took over, and she grabbed Cassidy's arm, her grip firm and unrelenting. Bringing a finger to her lips, she gestured for Cassidy to follow her to the door. Leaning against it, Dora strained to listen, while Cassidy rubbed her now-sore arm, muttering under her breath. Despite her irritation, she soon joined Dora, pressing her own ear to the door as well.

The footsteps and voices grew louder until they were just outside. A man's voice became discernible, his tone dismissive: "I'm leaving. No use hanging around. He's gone and taken the Englishman with him. If he plans to ransom him, he'll do it without us. We're not needed any more. There's gold been found on the far side of Devil's Mountain. I'm heading to the boarding house for the night, and in the morning, I'm off to make my fortune."

A second voice, sharper and angrier, interrupted. Cassidy recognized it as Ruth's. Though at first her words were indistinct, her voice soon rose, clear and biting.

"I know he killed my man and took off with Josh, but I'm sure he'll need my help. I'm staying right here, where he knows to find me. He can't write. I'm the one who wrote all the ransom notes. He'll come back here, mark my words."

"Why should he come back to you?" the man retorted. "He's got the Englishman. He can deal directly with his friends. All he has to do is send a message to the general store where Josh's friends gather, and they'll get the message soon enough. You're not needed any more."

"I *am* needed!" Ruth's anger flared, her voice rising further. "He needs me to handle the ransom deal, to arrange the gold for the exchange."

"You stupid woman. You were only useful when he had the boy. He didn't want to deal with a crying child while hiding out with his hostages. But now? Now, you're no longer useful. There's no money for you in this. You should've taken the Limey's offer and gone to England. Do what you want, Ruth. I'm off to strike it rich!"

Footsteps echoed down the hall, followed by the loud slam of the front door. Silence returned briefly before it was broken by the voice of the other woman who had been with Ruth.

"What are you going to do, Ruth?" she asked, her tone curious and cautious. Her question mirrored Cassidy's own thoughts as she pressed closer to the door, desperate not to miss Ruth's response.

Cassidy had recognized the voice. It was the voice of Lil, who had managed the boarding house in Duloe. Lil must believe there's money to be had, or she wouldn't have come with Ruth to Nowhere.

"I don't know," Ruth admitted after a pause. "But I'll tell you one thing. I want my share of the ransom money, and I want to kill that bitch Cassidy."

"But you heard what Red just said. She had nothing to do with your man's death," the other woman countered. "Your man was killed by the kidnapper himself. Cassidy is no fool. You're wasting your time going after her, or trying to get a share of the ransom money. He'll never give it to you. And Red's right, you were only needed to help with the boy. Now Red's gone off to the gold fields, and I'm going with him."

"What? You'd leave me here, with the promise of the ransom money I could get, to go with that man and dig for gold?" Ruth's voice rose in disbelief and fury.

"I'm not digging," the other woman retorted coolly. "He'll get me there safely, and I'll cook for the miners. That's where the real money is. Digging for gold is a fool's errand. Feeding them puts money in my pocket. I'm off to join him at the boarding house. If you had any sense at all, Ruth, you'd join me there. "

"Go, then!" Ruth shouted after her, her voice laced with fury, "And heaven help you, scratching in the dirt for gold in the ice and snow!"

The conversation ceased, and the hall fell silent once more. Cassidy glanced at Dora, her eyes wide with a mixture of relief and resolve. The fragmented words she had overheard confirmed her worst fears, but also provided the clues she needed to act. The perilous game she was caught in was far from over, but she now had a clearer picture of her enemies and their intentions. It was time to make her move!

Now she had a clearer picture of what was happening with Ruth and also the kidnapper. Ruth was no use whatsoever in getting Josh back safely. This new information was a vital clue. And Cassidy had made her decision.

CHAPTER FORTY-SIX

"What are you going to do?" Dora asked her. She walked away from the door and, standing in the middle of the room, stared at Cassidy who still stood behind the door,

Cassidy stood for a moment, thinking things through. "It's no use my staying here. Ruth is not in contact with the kidnapper. She's no help to me now. Her man is dead. There's nothing for it, Dora. Help me on with my coat!" Cassidy grabbed her coat from the back of the chair where she had flung it.

"Surely you won't leave now? Grey won't leave in the dark. I thought you said he would stay overnight at the livery stable and check the weather in the morning. If the weather promises less snow, then he'll get going up Devil's Mountain."

"Yes, but how will I let him know I want to go with him? I won't be able to join him unless I leave now. And then there's Ruth. I don't want her to know I've been here. I don't want to fight her. It could turn nasty between us if she saw me here. "

The thought of the two women coming to blows, and the amount of blood that could be shed by them, made Dora cringe inwardly. It had taken a lot of time, money, and care to get her hotel up and running and looking as good as it did. Her carpets, her freshly painted walls and her furniture would not survive a battle between Cassidy and Ruth. Without another word, Dora picked up the coat and held it up for Cassidy to shrug herself into.

"Before you go, let me make up some food for you," Dora offered, feeling guilty about pushing Cassidy out into the snow because she didn't want her hotel to become the macabre scene of a shoot-out.

"No need, Dora. If I know Grey in his office and down at the livery stable, there will be plenty of food. Grey always makes certain that he has plenty of coffee and provisions whenever he wants them. I don't understand how he manages it, but the man has a knack."

The side window of the hotel was opened, and Cassidy prepared to slip through it. Turning back, she kissed Dora on the cheek. "Look after yourself, Dora. That woman Ruth needs to be watched."

"It's you that needs to look after yourself, Cassidy. Fancy climbing a mountain in thick snow after violent criminals. Cassidy, I think you are mad!"

As Dora closed the window, the soft chuckle from Cassidy drifted back to her as she walked along the sidewalk. Her slim figure, swamped in the heavy sheepskin coat, soon disappeared in the swirling snowflakes.

"What are you doing here?" Grey asked as she pushed the office door closed behind her, struggling against the snowy wind blowing outside. The door of his office banged shut, and he winced. There was already a mark on the wall where Cassidy, in her usual haste, had crashed it open many times before.

"Coffee, Cassidy?" He walked over to the stove to pour out the coffee for her.

After what she had just told him about the conversation between Ruth and her fellow conspirators, he was lost in deep thought.

Climbing out of the window to avoid them made him smile. Cassidy had turned it into a joke. She laughed. He was unaware of why he was smiling back at her, but no one could ignore that smile. Her violet eyes widened, crinkling at the corners, and sparkling with merriment.

Her mouth curved with a slight tendency for one corner to lift higher than the other. Grey felt himself being drawn into those eyes, and for a moment, he wondered what it would be like if he let himself go. Then, taking a firm hold of the coffeepot, he poured her a steaming hot mug.

"I thought you might have gone to the livery stable," Cassidy said, as she cupped her hands around the hot tin mug, relishing the warmth it gave to her chilly fingers.

"No, not yet. I'm sorting out some paperwork and thought I'd spend the night here to give the deputy some time off before I head up to the mountain."

The papers on his desk included drawings, descriptions, and some dusty, faded-looking photographs.

"New wanted posters?" Cassidy asked, walking over to join him and looking down at the desk as he shuffled the papers.

"Yes, just in from Duloe. So, you haven't answered me. Why are you here, Cassidy? I thought you'd be at the hotel waiting for a ransom note."

While they both examined the papers, pushing one evil-looking face aside and picking up another, Cassidy explained more fully what had happened at the hotel.

"I thought it best I left. That Ruth worries me. I think she's crazy. I don't want any trouble when it's not needed."

"That's a first! That is definitely a first—Cassidy avoiding trouble."

Her head whipped up, and she glared at him. At his laughing smile, she relented and smiled back.

The next poster he moved to one side, but before he laid it down, Cassidy grabbed it. "That's the man who was with Ruth tonight. So, he's wanted, is he? That makes sense. Have you any idea if he's in a gang or anything?"

Grey continued reading the poster, then nodded. "Yes, he runs with the Briggs gang. That must be who masterminded the kidnapping of Josh. Ruth must be involved with the gang, and that's how Josh and Charlie's kidnap happened. They saw an opportunity to hold them for ransom, after Ruth told them of Josh's plans."

"What about the woman?" Cassidy asked as Grey paused by the door. "If you capture him, what will *she* do?"

CHAPTER FORTY-SEVEN

Grey hesitated, his hand resting on the doorframe. "I reckon she'll go back to the hotel or maybe head back again to the boarding house at the other end of town."

"I'll stay here, then," Cassidy said, her voice firm.

"Go into my room, wait there, and stay out of sight." Grey instructed before stepping out and shutting the door behind him. A swirl of snowflakes swept in, scattering onto the floor before vanishing in the warmth radiating from the stove.

Cassidy refilled her coffee mug and took a sip as she moved toward Grey's private room. The sheriff's office had always struck her as a peculiar setup. The jail cell at the back had only just been fitted with proper window bars. A scuffle between Grey and the blacksmith months earlier had left the cell window damaged and unusable for some time, much to the dismay of the townsfolk. The idea of criminals roaming free because of faulty locks and no bars had made everyone uneasy. Now there was a new blacksmith in Nowhere, and the bars had been fixed. Finally!

The main office was functional, with a desk, a few chairs and the equipment necessary for a sheriff needed to run a frontier town. But Grey's private room was new. Built as an addition when he assumed the position, it served as his personal retreat—a place he could be found at any hour of the day or night. No one, as far as Cassidy knew, had ever entered that room. The prospect of being one of the first to step inside stirred a mixture of curiosity and unease.

Determined, yet somehow hesitant, she pushed open the door. A faint shouting from the livery stable outside caught her attention. Grabbing a small oil lamp from a shelf in the main office, she entered Grey's private quarters, peering out a small, curtained window.

The snow was still falling in thick, heavy flakes, obscuring much of the street. Through the swirling white, she could make out Grey, standing firm as he exchanged words with a woman. The deputy held a man in his grip, shoving him toward the boardwalk in front of the sheriff's office. The woman's angry gestures were clear, even from a distance. After a final, sharp retort, she stormed off down Main Street, disappearing past the hotel into the snowy darkness.

"She's heading for the boarding house," Cassidy murmured, taking another sip of coffee. At least the livery stable would be now safe, without the chance of Ruth or her friend arriving. The noise of boots stomping snow off them filled the sheriff's office. Cassidy listened as the three men entered, their voices loud and angry. The prisoner was protesting his innocence, but his complaints were abruptly silenced. She guessed he'd been shown a wanted poster with his face on it. Footsteps echoed as they led him to the cell.

A moment later, Grey's voice called out, "Reckon you can head to the livery stable now, Cassidy!" Before leaving the room, she took a quick glance around it. Sparsely furnished, a single bed was against one wall. There was a small table, a chair, and, most surprising of all, a bookshelf. Longing to see what the books were on it, Cassidy couldn't spare the time. Grey was outside, waiting for her. Later, she thought, later I will think about what I saw in his room and how it gives me an insight into the enigmatic man that is Grey. She left the room.

Cassidy set her mug down on the desk, placed the

lamp beside it, and paused. The deputy emerged from the cell, his grizzled face splitting into a broad smile. He was clearly pleased at the prospect of earning the bounty.

"You're mad," he muttered, shaking his head as he glanced between Grey and Cassidy. "Anyone going out anywhere in this weather is crazy. Look at it out there! You can't see a hand in front of your face, let alone make it up the mountain. Best wait till morning, see if the worst of the storm's passed. Even then, it'll be a hard climb." He looked from one to the other, shaking his head, before walking to the stove and warming his hands in front of it. He shook his head yet again. "Mad, that's what you two are, crazy mad!"

Grey raised an eyebrow at Cassidy. "What do you think? Still going?" His dark face held no expression as he looked at the petite woman in front of him. Grey never doubted her spirit, but he wondered if the thought of this journey to Devil's Mountain during the tail end of a blizzard would be too much for her.

"We'll get to the livery stable now," she replied. "Give it an hour or two, then let's hope we can leave by dawn."

Snuggling into her heavy coat, she pulled the collar high, rammed her hat onto her head, and opened the door. The wind struck her with brutal force, almost pushing her back into the office. For a moment, she staggered, but she steadied herself and pressed forward. Battling against the gale, she managed, with Grey's help, to shut the door behind her. Behind them, they could hear the voice of the deputy as he said again, "Crazy mad, that's what you two are!"

The boardwalk offered little shelter as the wind howled, driving snow against her face and coat. Struggling onward, Cassidy kept her head down, gripping the hitching rails along the boardwalk, and they finally reached the stable and shoved the door open.

Snow followed them in, swirling and stinging. They fought to close the door against the wind, until a powerful pair of hands from behind them finally pushed it shut. Turning, Cassidy looked up into Sam's laughing face.

"You look like a snowman," he said with a grin. "Come in, Cassidy. Get closer to the stove and let's get you warm and dry."

CHAPTER FORTY-EIGHT

The sudden loud creak of the door startled everyone. In an instant, pistols appeared in the hands of all present in the stable, save for the old man who had settled down on his bed and was snoring, oblivious to the commotion.

"Sam, it's me! Let me in!" came a desperate whisper from outside the door. Recognizing the voice, Sam rushed to unbolt the stable door, allowing one of his Apache cousins to slip inside. The man was crusted with snow, his face pale, and trembling from the bitter cold that had accompanied him on his journey. He rushed toward the brazier, stretching his hands out to the fire and exhaling a tremendous sigh of relief.

"It's bad. Didn't know if I'd make it," he muttered through chattering teeth. Without hesitation, one of the group helped him remove his coat, while another handed him a steaming tin mug of coffee. The Apache grasped it gratefully, his blue-tinged hands clutching the warmth it provided.

After taking a few sips, he gave a deep sigh and addressed the group. "I followed them. Josh is still alive. They're holding him for ransom. More gold. But the weather's the real problem. They've taken him to Old Gabe's cabin in the hidden valley near the abandoned mine."

Exclamations came from each one of them, varying from those that were delighted Josh was still alive and those worried about how they were going to rescue him.

The man paused, sipping his coffee again as he continued to warm his hands. His shivering had subsided, and the bluish hue of his face was fading.

"How many men are with him?" Grey asked. Cassidy

could see that his brain was working already. She knew Grey was figuring out how to rescue Josh, whether they could reach him in this weather. She knew Grey was thinking about these things, because she was also calculating what they should do next.

"One other was with him when the guys reached the cabin. He picked up another man in Duloe Town, and together they struggled to get Josh to the cabin safely. So that's one man with Josh and the kidnapper." He paused for another sip. "But the snow is thick around that cabin. It'd be difficult to reach them without being seen against the brightness of the snow."

"Can we get to Reuben's cave?" Cassidy asked. If they could reach the cave, Cassidy thought that would be one step closer to Josh. Then, when the weather loosed its hold on the canyons and valleys, they would be nearer to the kidnappers than if they remained in Nowhere.

"Yes," came the reply, though hesitantly. "But I don't know how long it'll remain accessible. If you go, you'll need provisions for a long stay. If it snows any more or freezes hard, the mountain up around Gabe's cabin will be impassable."

A heavy silence fell over the group as they digested his words, contemplating the monumental task ahead. They had to rescue Josh, but the odds were stacked against them.

"Do you think they know you were following them?" Grey asked.

"No. They weren't looking behind or taking any precautions. They don't think anyone would dare follow them in this weather."

Grey nodded thoughtfully. "If we could catch up to them in this snow, do you think we'd stand a chance of rescuing Josh? If he has only one man with him, we stand a good chance, and we would have the element of surprise on our side. There would be no time for him to get reinforcements."

Cassidy was surprised. Grey rarely sought advice, which only added to the enigmatic air that surrounded him. She realized there was more to Grey than the stoic mask he presented to the world. He was a man of many faces, a chameleon who could shift between roles: a preacher, a sheriff, or a man of the wilderness. She found herself intrigued by the layers he kept hidden, much like her own guarded persona. But there was no time to dwell on such thoughts. They needed rest before embarking on what would undoubtedly be a gruelling journey.

Before dawn, they set off. Each had snatched what little sleep they could beforehand. Coffee was brewed, cold biscuits were eaten, and provisions were packed into saddlebags. Cassidy smiled as she noticed the coffee tucked securely into Grey's saddlebag. The group rode out of Duloe Town under a dark sky, the faint shafts of moonlight barely illuminating the snowy landscape. Only the faintest sliver of light could be seen above Devil's mountain, the sign that dawn was breaking.

Suddenly, a gunshot shattered the stillness. A second shot followed almost immediately. Grey spun around to see a woman standing in an alley, a pistol aimed at Cassidy. Cassidy's horse reared, and she fell into the snow, lying motionless. The woman let out a wild laugh. "I told you I'd kill her! I know she had something to do with my man's death. Now I've gone and killed her!"

Sam hurled himself from his horse. He ran over to the woman, disarmed her and dragged her, still laughing wildly, toward the sheriff's office. A sleepy deputy emerged, rifle in hand, staring open mouthed at the scene in front of him.

After the shot, Grey leapt from his horse and flung himself beside Cassidy, dread filling his heart. He turned her over, expecting to find her grievously wounded. Instead, her violet eyes flicked open, sparkling with mischief. The lopsided smile she gave him made him want to kiss her. It took all his strength of will to just smile back down at her.

"Are you hurt?" he asked, his hands trembling as they searched for injuries.

"No," she replied, laughter bubbling up. "She only hit the sleeve of my coat. I pretended to be dead so she wouldn't fire again."

Grey stared at her in disbelief. He sat back on his haunches, unable to believe what she was saying. "You're unharmed? Not even a scratch?"

"Not even a little scratch," she said with a grin. "Help me up, though. This coat is soaked with snow, and I can't move."

Grey extended his hand, pulling her to her feet. Relief washed over him, and he found himself holding her close to him for a moment. "I thought you were dead," he admitted. "It looked as if she had killed you, with just the one shot."

Cassidy chuckled, the mischievous glint in her eyes as she looked up at him, making him smile back down at her. "It's a trick I've used before. Works every time." She glanced toward the sheriff's office, where the woman was being led away, still screaming and laughing.

Then another shot echoed down Main Street. The group, now on horseback, turned round to face the sheriff's office. Stumbling out the door, the deputy sheriff waved a hand at them. His voice quavering a little, reached them as he shouted. "She grabbed my gun! Turned it on herself. She's dead!"

No one spoke. There was little to say. Grey gave a shrug and looked at Cassidy. She shook her head and snuggled back down into the coat. The woman had betrayed Josh and little Charlie. Cassidy spared her no sympathy or any further thoughts.

The group gathered themselves and resumed their journey. The snow had stopped, and the faint dawning light provided some visibility. Thoughts of the task ahead filled their minds as they rode on, their breath visible in the freezing air. Cassidy's thoughts lingered on Josh. on the man who had lost so much but still had a son waiting for him.

The frozen landscape stretched before them, unyielding and treacherous, as they pressed on toward Reuben's cave. It began snowing again.

CHAPTER FORTY-NINE

Josh watched as the tiny figure of Charlie, his son, was swept up onto Cassidy's horse. The hesitation of the horse as she settled down with the boy in front of her was only momentary. Within what seemed like twenty seconds, she rode off. The speed of the horse increased, and for a brief moment, the figure on the horse twisted around to look at him. Even at that distance, Josh could see the anguish etched on Cassidy's face.

Josh unclenched his jaw and released the tension in his hands, which had been gripped into fists. He felt a small measure of relief seeing his son whisked away to safety. He knew Charlie would be safe with Cassidy. She would fight like a vixen to keep him safe.

"Not sorry to see the kid go," the man behind him sneered. "Definitely no need for that Ruth now. No need for her to write those fancy letters demanding ransom."

Josh said nothing. He knew better than to respond. The bruises and cuts on his face showed that. "Least said, soonest mended," the old adage sprang to his mind, unbidden. Where had that come from? he wondered. His thoughts were a tangled mess, a haze of disjointed phrases and flickers of people and places that vanished as quickly as they appeared. For instance, he had no memory of a wife who had borne him a son and died in childbirth. No recollection of a marriage at all. But Charlie had arrived—his son. His first sight of his small son, Charlie, had been looking at a miniature image of himself. The same floppy blond hair, the same blue eyes had looked straight at him with puzzlement. There was no denying that he was Josh's son. During their imprisonment together, Josh had tried to talk to the boy, trying to build a relationship with him. But it hadn't worked. The small child, newly arrived in his life, had remained quiet and withdrawn throughout their captivity together.

***

"I've got the gold. It's all mine now," Buck growled, kicking the lifeless body lying before them. "Didn't trust him at all. Him and that woman, Ruth, scheming against me. I knew they were. Now he's dead, and Ruth can stay rotting in Duloe, waiting for his return."

He strode over to his horse and, with care, tucked the gold into his saddlebags. Josh stood, stunned. One moment, it seemed he was on the brink of freedom, with ransom to be paid for him and Charlie. Now, here he was, still a captive. Josh didn't know the right word for it. Was he now a prisoner? Hostage? Pawn? Whatever it was, he knew that with his hands bound and a gun often trained on him, escape seemed impossible. Still, a faint flicker of hope stirred within him. Ever since their capture, Josh had done nothing to jeopardize Charlie's safety. His son's welfare had been his only priority. But now, with Charlie gone, a new determination within him formed.

Standing by while Ruth had fawned over his son, pretending kindness while betraying them both, had been excruciating. How could she do it? How could she smile so sweetly at Charlie while leading him into the hands of these ruthless men? Josh knew she had been infatuated with one of them, the man now lying dead at Buck's feet. Ruth would wait for his return in vain. Was it wrong of him to feel that Ruth had perhaps brought it upon herself?

"Get up on the horse," Buck barked at Josh. "We're heading toward Nowhere. The weather's bad, but I know a place where we can hole up. Someone I can trust. I can send him for more ransom money."

Some hours later, they arrived at a small ramshackle cabin on the outskirts of Nowhere. Wearily, Josh dismounted and followed his captor inside. The cabin's interior was dim and cold, with an air of neglect. An old woman stood by the small fire, stirring something in a large pot. She didn't look up when they entered, and Josh realized she must be deaf. When she turned to face them, her expression was inscrutable, though her eyes flickered with apprehension. She set two more plates on the rough-hewn table without a word.

"What happened?" a man seated by the fire demanded, leaping to his feet as Buck entered.

Buck tossed his hat onto the table and sank down on a chair. "Got the gold. Still got one captive. Hoping to squeeze another pot of gold out of them for him. The boy's gone, though, escaped with a woman. As for your friend, he argued with me. Nobody questions my judgment and lives."

Buck began eating the stew placed before him, oblivious to the tension in the room. Josh sat at the table as well, murmuring thanks to the old woman as she set a plate in front of him. He didn't know what was in the stew, but he didn't care. Hot, tasteless, with lumpy vegetables floating around in it—but he ate it. He needed the strength it would give him. Josh's thoughts turned to Charlie. The boy's safety was all that mattered. No longer worried about Charlie, his main effort would be to endure whatever it took to ensure they would be reunited.

The man seated by the fire, clearly nervous, glanced at Buck. "This cabin ... You say it's in a hidden valley? We'll be safe there until spring?" The death of his friend at Buck's hand had frightened him, taking him by surprise. The distrust he now felt for Buck was apparent to Josh's intent gaze.

Buck nodded. "We'll head out as soon as the storm lets up. Pack up all the provisions you can find here."

The old woman protested softly as they emptied her shelves of food. Josh, seeing her distress, slipped a bag of flour and a small packet of coffee, and one of beans, onto the floor, where she could retrieve them. Her eyes met his, and she gave a slight nod of thanks.

Again, they mounted their horses and set off into the blizzard.

CHAPTER FIFTY

When they set off again, the blizzard had worsened. The snow was no longer powdery but dense and sticky, clinging to everything it touched. The horses' movements grew labored, their hooves sinking deeply into the snow. Josh could see the strain in their eyes and the frosty puffs of their breaths. Buck's impatience grew as they struggled to make progress.

"How much longer before we reach this valley?" Mick shouted over the wind.

"Not far now," Buck called back. "I just need to find the scarred cactus. That's the marker."

Josh's heart lifted. He knew this terrain well. With the carpet of deep snow and the whirling snowflakes, Josh had ridden on without recognizing the landmarks. Now, he looked about him, peering through the drifting snow. The scarred cactus was a landmark he and Amy had often visited, its distinctive silhouette etched in his memory. As they neared the cactus, Josh's mind began to race. He knew the way to Old Gabe's cabin from here. That must be where Buck was heading. It was a long tricky journey, Josh remembered.

But Josh also knew the path to Reuben's cave. It was a treacherous route that could provide an opportunity for his escape. Could he dare to attempt it on his own, without the help of the others, to guide him and lead the way? He had sheltered there in the past with Amy, Reuben and Martha. Hidden from view, the secret of it had been given to Reuben by an old miner he had befriended. A steep cliff path led up to a tiny valley with a small spring and a cave giving shelter. Remembering their last visit, Josh knew provisions were always left there for their future visits. If he could reach it, there would be water and wood piled high beside a fireplace in the cave itself, alongside tinned provisions. If he could get there, he would be away from Buck, and could wait the blizzard out.

Could he cope with the steep cliff path up to the cave? Josh hated heights, and had always gone up and down with the reassurance of Amy, or Sam, or Reuben with him. Could he cope with that perilous ledge on his own in a blizzard? Did he have any choice?

When they paused at a small overhang for shelter, Josh saw his chance.

"My hands are freezing. I'll get frostbite if you don't untie them." He held up his hands blue and white with the cold and lack of movement.

"Best untie him, Mick—he's no good for a ransom with no hands!" Buck roared with laughter at this joke, slapping his own hands on his thighs.

The ropes were cut away by Mick, and Josh began trying to get the circulation going in his hands again. He walked over to the horse he was riding on and stood beside it for a moment and then went to the mule they had stolen from the old woman.

Under the guise of tending to his freezing hands, he pocketed some biscuits, bacon and coffee from the provisions. His hands burned as the blood returned to them, but he ignored the pain. The wind beyond the overhang had lessened, but the cold remained biting.

As they got ready to press on, the storm cleared for a moment, revealing the jagged outlines of the cliffs and peaks of Devil's Mountain ahead. Josh's mind raced. If he could slip away unnoticed, he might reach Reuben's cave and find shelter. The plan was dangerous, but it was his only option. Clenching his fists, he whispered a silent prayer and prepared to act.

"This horse is going lame," Josh shouted out, bending down and inspecting the leg of his mount but shielding it from the view of the others. There was nothing wrong with the horse. "It'll be better if I ride the mule and let the horse carry the lighter loads."

"Yes, do it then, but be quick about it!" Buck shouted at him. Gazing around at the worsening weather, Buck was only too anxious to make a move and didn't bother to check the horse himself.

Josh fumbled clumsily with the provisions, trying to transfer them from the mule to the horse. His hands were still stiff and awkward after the rope had tied them. Buck, irritated by the delay, shouted at him again, "Get on the mule! It can carry your weight as well as that load. We have no time to waste. This weather's getting worse by the minute. We've still a long way to the cabin, and I'll be damned if I'm going to be out here after dark!"

Josh, feeling the sting of Buck's acid tone, handed the lead rope of the horse he had been riding to Mick and climbed onto the mule without a second thought. He knew better than to argue. The man could reply with a blow and the gun, as well as words. The mule, sturdy and dependable, still carried flour, beans, and other packages wrapped in cloth, their contents unknown to him. Josh felt a strange lightheartedness creeping over him despite the grim circumstances. It wasn't joy, but a fleeting sense of opportunity. This was his moment to break away. He slumped on the mule, careful not to let his face betray his thoughts, and followed the others into the canyon. A mule would carry him with a sure-footed gait up the path. He was certain he had heard somewhere that they were more reliable than a horse. Josh patted the neck of his new friend the mule and hoped his trust in it would not be a mistake.

Buck, ever impatient, led the group, urging his horse ever faster, his breath visible in the icy air. Mick trailed behind, his eyes scanning the path, with Buck ahead and Josh at the rear, his mind churning. He glanced around at the snow piling up in drifts along the canyon walls. It fell, blanketing the world in white and muffling all sound. Despite the peril, a small smile almost broke through his tense expression.

"This might be my only chance," he thought, the absurdity of the situation not lost on him. "Maybe it's a stupid mistake, but if I don't do it, I'll regret it forever."

He took a deep, deliberate breath, holding it for a moment before releasing it. "Keep calm. Keep calm," he murmured to himself. This might be his only chance to escape to safety. The snow piled into ever higher drifts along the canyon walls, and the relentless fall of flakes cloaked the landscape. Josh almost laughed aloud at his folly. "My only chance," he thought. "It's a fool's move. But I'm going to act, and now!"

CHAPTER FIFTY-ONE

Josh had a plan. His actions in carrying out this plan may well be fatal. But he had no reliance on surviving captivity with Buck. The man had gold already from Cassidy. Josh was certain he had more stashed away in Old Gabe's cabin. Even if he survived Buck's erratic behavior and was ransomed again, there was no certainty that he and the other men would survive this weather, the journey to the cabin, or even a stay there. He'd been told about the strange triangular rock marking the hidden path to a secluded valley. Reuben had often spoken of the old miner who'd lived there, hidden away in a tiny hollow. The miner had been grateful for Reuben's help over the years, especially for hauling supplies up the treacherous cliff-side path. Josh remembered following Reuben along the cliff edge in better weather, terrified of the heights but reassured by Reuben's steady guidance. That had been in spring, with sunshine and the scent of blooming flowers in the air. Now, in a blizzard, with an unfamiliar mule beneath him, Josh doubted his courage. Could he do it? Could he, terrified of heights, manage alone?

Ahead, the triangular rock came into view, its snow-covered sides shedding their icy coating to reveal its unmistakable shape. It stood out as if placed there. Josh swallowed hard, slowing the mule's pace until he fell behind Buck and Mick. The blizzard engulfed them in a white haze. Almost without conscious thought, Josh turned the mule's head toward the narrow path leading upward. He looked back and saw the figures of Buck and Mick continuing forward and disappearing into the falling snow. They hadn't thought to look behind. Buck never expected him to try to escape in this severe weather. But he'd done it. He was on his own. The way ahead with his new friend, the mule, was in front of him.

Josh's ascent was gruelling. The path was narrow, with a sheer drop on one side that made Josh's head swim. When the snow swirled in gusts of wind, the valley below disappeared from his anxious gaze. Josh was grateful that he could no longer see it. The mule climbed, its hooves finding purchase with an almost uncanny precision. Josh whispered words of encouragement to the beast, his voice trembling with fear. "If we make it up there, you'll find shelter, warmth and rest," he murmured, patting the mule's neck. He knew it was foolish to talk to the animal as if it understood, but the act steadied his nerves.

At last, they reached the ledge that signaled the entrance to the hidden valley. Josh's legs felt weak as he dismounted, and he slumped against the mule for support. They had made it. Relief flooded through him, mingling with the bone-deep exhaustion that now gripped him.

The valley looked familiar, yet was transformed under the heavy snow. Josh recognized landmarks, though it took effort to distinguish them beneath the white blanket. He guided the mule toward the trickling spring near the back wall of the valley, relieved to find it still flowing. Sliding from the mule's back, he coaxed the animal through a narrow opening into a sheltered cave. Inside, the air was icy but—mercifully—still dry.

Josh's frozen hands fumbled as he reached for a tin box containing matches. Striking one, he lit a candle, the small flame casting a warm glow on the cave walls. He spotted a pile of kindling and firewood left by the cave's previous occupant. Grateful for their foresight, he soon built a fire. Its warmth filled the cavern space, lifting the oppressive chill.

The mule stood quietly as Josh removed its saddle and unpacked the provisions, placing them on a rocky ledge near the fire. He examined the animal's back, wincing at the sight of sores left untreated. Gently, he cleaned them with snow, easing the mule's discomfort. Then he ventured deeper into the cave, searching for food. On a shelf carved into the cave rock, he found the provisions left by Martha: corned beef, tomatoes and canned fruit were among the items, much to his delight.

That night, for the first time since his kidnapping, Josh slept deeply. Charlie was safe. He knew Amy would look after him. He had escaped from Buck. No longer was he at the mercy of that unstable man. If he survived the blizzard in the cave, all would be well. The future, he didn't care about—not at the moment. It was enough to know that both he and Charlie were safe. The fear and tension that had gripped him for days finally loosened their hold. Wrapped in a blanket, he lay near the fire, its steady crackle a soothing backdrop to his dreams.

The next morning, Josh awoke to the mule's restless snorting. His body protested as he moved, stiff and sore from the cold. Slowly, he rekindled the fire's embers and prepared a pot of coffee. The snow had stopped, and daylight filtered into the cave, illuminating the icy landscape outside. Josh led the mule to the spring for water and cleared a patch of snow to reveal green grass. Josh felt another flicker of hope. He was alive and free from Buck. But Buck still had the papers and the journal. Kept by Ruth and stolen from his brother, Josh knew it held secrets and details hidden away from his empty memory. Buck had taunted him with them, telling him they would cost extra gold for him to have them.

But for now Josh could only feel relief at his freedom and the thought of his breakfast by the fire.

CHAPTER FIFTY-TWO

Cassidy rode through the snow, bundled in her borrowed coat. The wind was still strong and snowflakes blew in sudden gusts into her face. The wind was still chilly, but huddled in the coat, she didn't feel it. Cassidy followed Grey and Sam, her resolve unwavering despite the treacherous conditions. They were all determined to retrieve Josh from his captors, but Cassidy had her own selfish motive. She was reclaiming the gold stolen from her. The kidnapper's crimes, his violence, and the cold-blooded murder of his companion had only solidified her determination. That gold had been earned by her years of bounty hunting. There had been danger, hardship, and fear endured—all to give her security for her life ahead. There was no way she was going to allow a man as evil and despicable as Buck to ride off with her gold!

The snow eased, falling in lighter flakes as Sam pointed toward the base of the ridge. "That's where Reuben's cave should be," he said, his voice low. The climb looked dangerous, as always, the path narrow and slick, but they didn't have another option. Not once had Cassidy traveled on that path without fear of tumbling down the jagged rock face to the canyon floor below. But those journeys had been done in sunlight, in pleasant weather. Even the times when it had been raining had been easier than the blizzard they were now facing. The horse she was riding had been capable on the journey. She didn't know this horse, and wondered how it would react to their journey up the narrow path in a snowstorm.

Sam led them toward Reuben's cave. The ascent was perilous, but Cassidy, reciting childhood prayers, trusted her horse to navigate the path. It was slow progress. At each bend, Sam paused before he ventured further on up the cliff face. Snow-laden gusts of wind whipped at their faces, and Cassidy turned her head away from the wind and the enormous drop beneath her.

She felt rather than saw the path widen before her. Wiping the snow from her face, Cassidy looked about her. Yes, relief flooded through her. They had reached the top of the path. Safety in the flat area above the tiny valley was now in front of her. She gave a pat to the horse that had valiantly struggled through the snow in unknown territory.

Sam had come to a halt. He raised his hand to signal them to halt. "Don't speak," he whispered.

Grey and Cassidy maneuvered their horses beside him. Neither spoke, but both looked at him, a question on both their faces.

"See, down there at the cave. I see the glow of a fire. Someone is in that cave!" Sam whispered as he got down from his horse, handing the reins to Grey. "I'll go down and see who it is."

His figure became a shadow as he carefully hugged the dark, looming places beneath the canyon walls. They could see him approach the entrance to the cave. Unable to see in the cave itself without revealing his presence, Sam climbed to an overhanging ledge, which looked straight into the cave itself.

"Cassidy, let's get down and walk toward the cave ourselves. We need shelter, and our horses are exhausted. No matter who is in the cave, we have to join them," Grey said and looked up at Cassidy.

"Yes, I couldn't have gone any further, and the horses are spent," Cassidy agreed with him and tumbled off her horse.

"Whoa there, are you all right, Cassidy?" Grey's strong arm grabbed her before she fell, face first, into the snow.

"My legs have gone to sleep. They can hardly hold me up," Cassidy said, and as quietly as possible, with one eye on Sam at the cave mouth, she began moving her feet and rubbing her legs.

On reaching a ledge where he could see into the cave entrance, Sam had paused. Cassidy saw his figure turn into an immobile statue. Snow coated his jacket, and even his features as it fell heavily onto him. Still, he watched, heedless of the cold and discomfort.

By this time, Sam could look into the cave. They could see him stiffen as a figure moved in front of the fire. A log must have been thrown on the fire as a sudden flare of flame and sparks came out of the cave mouth. A movement within it cast long shadows out of the cave onto the snow. Then, as the two watchers stared intently, Sam rose to his feet. He walked forward to peer into the cave itself.

Sam stiffened. He wiped the snow away from his face as if it had been blinding him. Those watching could see him look again and again.

"What is it? What can Sam see? Who's in the cave?" Grey whispered in Cassidy's ear as they cautiously approached the front of the cave.

"I think we ought to be ready," Cassidy whispered back, easing her gun from the pocket of the huge sheepskin coat. She noticed Grey had his gun in his hand, and both stood motionless, guns ready for action.

Taking a deep breath, Cassidy moved closer to Grey, her gun ready.

They both watched Sam as he moved forward to get a

better view of the person moving around in the cave.

"What can he see?" Cassidy whispered.

"Not what he can see, but *who* is it he can see?" Grey whispered back.

CHAPTER FIFTY-THREE

"It's Josh!" Sam shouted, his voice filled with astonishment and relief. Sam turned and waved to Grey and Cassidy and shouted again. "It's Josh in the cave! Come and see—it's Josh!"

Cassidy stumbled after Grey, the long sheepskin coat catching between her legs, and she struggled to stay upright between it and the deep snow.

Josh, hearing Sam's shout from within the cave, had rushed to the entrance. "Sam! Is that really you? What are you doing here? It's good to see you!"

Rushing to the cave entrance, Josh could hardly believe his eyes. Struggling through the heavy snow toward him came the Apache, his head and shoulders caked with snow. But the smile on Sam's handsome face, with his high cheekbones, was no illusion.

Pushing past Sam, the tall figure of Grey, no longer clad in black, rushed toward him. Snow caked his tall, thin figure, and with outstretched hands he reached Josh. "Are you on your own? How did you get here, Josh? What's happened?" The questions came from Grey as he rushed up to shake Josh's hand again and again.

Struggling to keep up with the two men, her smaller steps and shorter legs finding the heavy depth of snow a struggle to plough through, Cassidy joined the small group. Cassidy said nothing. She just lifted the huge coat with one hand and rushed headlong at Josh. Letting go of her coat, she flung her arms around him and gave him an enormous hug. Almost swept back onto the ground by this sudden onslaught from Cassidy, Josh laughed and laughed, and swung her around, lifting her feet off the ground.

"I escaped!" Josh began talking, but was stopped by an icy finger on his lips.

"Later, Josh. Can we get into the warmth of the fire and see to our horses before we all collapse? We are so cold and tired." Cassidy's plaintive voice cut through the celebratory comments of the men.

"Come on! Come into the cave," Josh said and turned to lead them in. He and Sam took the horses' reins, leading them through to the inner cave where the horses were normally kept.

Looking back over his shoulder, Josh shouted to Grey, "There's fresh coffee just made in the pot by the fire."

That evening, Josh felt content for the first time in weeks. Ever since his capture and the betrayal by Ruth of himself and Charlie, Josh had lived on his nerves. Sleep had been snatched in small periods. With Charlie by his side, he slept very little, constantly fearing imminent death for himself and his son. When Charlie had been rescued by Cassidy, the strain upon him was lessened. However, the actual fear of his kidnapper Buck had been worse after Buck killed his friend.

"And you rode away on the mule carrying all their provisions?" Grey said, stunned at Josh's tale of his escape. "Why did they let you go with all the stuff?" Grey stood by the fire, warming his backside, a tin mug of coffee in his hand. The largest tin mug he could find!

"I told them my horse was lame and I would go on the mule and transfer the provisions over to the horse. But Buck just yelled at me to climb on the mule and get going," Josh said and smiled at Sam, who was investigating each package in the pile Josh had put on their provision ledge.

"Shall I do the cooking tonight?" Sam said and began

bringing provisions over toward the fire.

"Yes please. I'm still frozen; I need to thaw out some more before I move," murmured Cassidy, who still snuggled in the coat. Her tiny hands clutched a mug of coffee while sipping it gratefully.

"I recognize that coat!" Josh exclaimed, taking a closer look at it. "That was Nancy's. I remember her wearing it."

"Amy gave it to me when we stopped off at Dry Creek Ranch. I was frozen on the journey to the ranch. This has been wonderful. It's kept me really warm all the way up here." At Josh's enquiring look, Cassidy continued speaking. "Charlie is fine, Josh. He's helping Amy and Flora with baby David. He's no longer in a suit, but wearing homemade dungarees and rushing about with the others!"

Josh smiled at this, and a little bit of the tension eased out of his body. If Charlie was doing well and enjoying himself, that was all to the good. He was fed well by Sam and Grey, who had combined their provisions with the kidnappers' supplies and those Josh had salvaged from the cave. Together, they created a hearty meal. The firewood they used was supplemented by a stash Josh had discovered earlier, on one of his excursions outside the cave. Hidden under a tarpaulin, the wood smoked slightly when first added to the fire but soon burned cleanly, radiating warmth. Secure in the company of his rescuers and assured of his son's safety at Dry Creek Ranch, Josh finally succumbed to a deep, restorative sleep.

While Josh slumbered, the others remained by the fire, its flickering light casting long shadows on the rocky walls. They spoke in hushed tones, careful not to disturb him.

"This changes everything," Grey began, clutching his tin coffee cup. "We no longer need to chase Buck to rescue Josh. Both captives are free now."

Sam's voice was firm, his words cutting through the Grey's comments. "I still want him dead. He's killed so many. Some were my cousins. They cry out for justice."

Cassidy nodded solemnly. "Buck will only continue killing if he's not stopped. But who's to say that Josh and Charlie were his only captives? There could be others held for ransom in that hut up in the mountain!"

CHAPTER FIFTY-FOUR

"Surely not," Grey replied, frowning. "Charlie and Josh were targets because they knew he had inherited a property and money in England. Do we know of anyone else who's gone missing?"

Both Sam and Cassidy shook their heads, but the grim possibility hung in the air. Grey shifted away from the fire as it flared up, the logs now blazing. "The important thing is to end Buck's reign of terror. Agreed?"

The others nodded. There was no need to wake Josh and ask him. The others knew what his answer would be. Silence in the cave fell upon the group as they thought of a possible gun battle ahead.

"We should capture him and take him in for trial," Grey continued, "but we know he'll fight to the death. The question is, when do we go after him?"

Sam, with his high cheekbones and sharp features illuminated by the firelight, looked resolute. "If we go now, we'll take him by surprise. Buck won't expect an attack in this weather. If we wait for better conditions, he'll be dug in and ready. And with Josh taking the mule and all its provisions, they may not have enough supplies to see them through this bad weather. We may find them weakened and only a few in number." It was a long speech for the normally reticent Sam.

Cassidy shivered in her sheepskin coat, and snuggled into the woollen rug she had put behind her against the cold, bare rock. "Can we even reach him in this weather? We barely made it to this cave. Climbing those icy trails to Gabe's cabin seems impossible to me."

All eyes turned back again to Sam. He knew the terrain and the weather. "Josh said Buck has one man with him. If the cabin has two more, that's four against us. With the element of surprise, we have the advantage. The blizzard's calming down, and by morning, it should be calm enough to travel through."

"Let's sleep on it. We'll check the weather tomorrow morning and make a decision then," Grey said and threw another log on the fire.

By the next morning, the snow had lessened, and the frost wasn't as severe as it had been. Sam's two cousins arrived with fresh provisions and game. After conferring with them, Sam turned and spoke to the others. "They followed Buck's tracks up to the cabin. It was him and Mick, and they think there were only another couple of men in the cabin itself. At the moment, the journey is passable up to the cabin. The snow is thick up there, but it's freezing hard and I think we ought to go now, before another blizzard comes in to the mountains. Clouds are gathering over the mountains. We may only have a short time to get up there before it snows again. "

"Coffee and some breakfast?" Grey said, moving toward the empty coffeepot.

"No—grab some cold biscuits, and we leave now. It's the only chance we have to get there in daylight," Sam replied. The urgency in his voice made the others rush to get ready for the journey ahead.

The group, after a hurried departure, soon struggled down the perilous ledge, collecting at the canyon entrance. Sam and his cousins had loaded up provisions in case they had to stay overnight. But Josh, Cassidy and Grey, exhausted by the last few days' exertions, had struggled to get ready and follow the Apache down the cliff-edge path.

The journey was begun, with Sam and his cousins

leading the way down the path. Josh was astonished to find that he had traveled down half of that cliff-edge path without even the slightest twinge of fear. I must be so exhausted with no energy left to be frightened, he thought to himself. He hid a smile as he looked at Cassidy, who was slumped over her horse, Nancy's sheepskin jacket wrapped around her, the collar up to her ears, and a shawl around her head. No one would ever mistake her at that moment for the elegant, stylish Rose Cassidy that turned heads when she walked down the streets of Duloe and Nowhere.

Grey, who was still grumbling about the lack of hot coffee, rode after the others as they carefully descended the icy ledge to the canyon floor. The sunrise painted the snow-covered landscape in hues of orange, red, and gold, but the beauty was lost on them. Their focus was on the mission ahead and navigating the path.

Not one of them thought that capturing Buck for trial was a possibility. No—they all knew that Buck would fight to evade the law and justice for his crimes. They had to be prepared for him to fight them to the death. Each one of them hoped it would be Buck's death, and not one of the group that was seeking to bring him to justice.

CHAPTER FIFTY-FIVE

Mid-morning found them at the mouth of Old Gabe's canyon. From their vantage point up on a ridge, they could see the cabin, its rough-hewn timbers weathered to a dark grey. Perched on a plateau halfway down, they could see wisps of smoke rising from its chimney. Footprints marked a trail from the cabin to the creek below, dark against the snow.

Sam scanned the area, his sharp eyes sweeping for movement. He huddled with the others behind a group of large boulders to plan the attack. "We'll split up," Sam decided. "The three of us"—he nodded toward his two cousins—"will circle around to cover the back and sides. Grey and Josh take the front and use that low ridge for cover. Cassidy, you'll cover the rear window. That way, no one will get out without us seeing them."

They nodded, grim determination in their eyes. Each of them checked their weapons, the metallic clicks sharp in the cold. Sam watched the others moving into place. Grey and Josh slipped toward the front, the figures low against the ridgeline. He could see Cassidy in position kneeling behind a bush, her gun trained on the cabin's rear window.

When everyone was in position, Sam gave the signal, a forward wave of his hand. The silence of the mountainside and the canyon were shattered. At Sam's signal, the three Indians let out bloodcurdling war cries, designed to draw the attention of those inside the cabin. There was a burst of activity inside the cabin. Shouts were accompanied by the crash of overturned furniture and the noise of heavy boots on wooden floors.

Then the gunfire started. Shots rang out from the

broken windows as rifles poked through the gaps, unleashing a hail of bullets toward the war cries. The Indians had already taken cover behind rocks and bushes. Their ploy had been successful in drawing out the kidnappers' fire.

With the defenders distracted, Grey and Josh seized their chance, charging down the snow-dusted slope toward the cabin. The crisp mountain air was split by the thunderous reports of their rifles, each shot echoing off the canyon walls like an incessant drumbeat. Their boots churned up the snow, the crunching noise loud despite the gunfire. A murky dark trail was left behind them in the snow as they advanced with grim determination.

Suddenly, the cabin door flew open with a violent crash. Buck burst out, dragging Mick in front of him like a makeshift shield. Mick's face was pale, his eyes wide with terror as he stumbled forward, losing his balance. Buck's voice bellowed over the chaos, a mixture of rage and desperation, though his words were drowned out by the relentless gunfire. The scene erupted into an uproar of noise as bullets tore through the frigid air, each crack and whine amplifying the tension.

The sharp bark of Grey's rifle forced Buck to falter for a split second. Sensing an opening, Mick twisted violently in Buck's grasp, trying to pull away, but Buck yanked him closer, using him again as cover.

The momentary distraction proved fatal. It was all the opening Grey needed. Grey's next shot struck true, and Buck staggered back with a guttural cry. His voice was raw with pain and fury. Buck clutched his side as crimson bloomed against his coat, his legs buckled beneath him, and he crumpled to the ground with a heavy thud, his breathing ragged and labored.

Inside the cabin, the remaining men scrambled to react, their panic clear. Moments later, three of them burst out of the cabin in a desperate bid for escape. They ran toward their horses tethered nearby. The sound of their shouts was soon drowned out by the relentless barrage from Grey and Josh.

"Don't let them reach the horses!" Josh shouted, his voice raw and urgent. "They mustn't escape!"

Grey didn't answer. His focus was absolute, his rifle steady despite the pounding of his heart. The fleeing men were easy targets against the pale expanse of snow. Grey gave out a deep breath as he repeatedly fired. One by one, they fell, their bodies collapsing into the snow in grotesque stillness. Blood seeped into the white expanse, stark and vivid against the cold winter light. The last man made it within arm's reach of a saddle, his fingers brushing the leather reins, before a single, perfectly placed shot from Josh ended his flight. He toppled to the ground with a lifeless thud.

The echoes of gunfire waned, leaving an eerie silence in their wake. Grey and Josh stood motionless for a moment, their breaths coming in ragged gasps in the frigid air. The snow-covered battlefield was littered with the still forms of their enemies, a grim testament to the violence that had just unfolded.

"Check Mick," Grey said, his voice low but firm. He didn't take his eyes off the cabin, his rifle still raised and ready.

Josh nodded and crept toward the trembling figure sprawled in the snow. Mick's face was streaked with blood and sweat, but his eyes met Josh's with a glimmer of relief.

"It's over," Josh murmured. And it was: Mick gave a

sigh and fell back, lifeless.

Josh stared for a moment, then turned away, his expression grim. "He's gone," he said quietly.

As silence fell, snow began to drift gently, covering the lifeless forms. Grey scanned his companions. "Anyone hurt?" he called.

One by one, they shook their heads, exhaustion and relief etched into their faces. Grey's shoulders relaxed, though his eyes remained wary. Grey approached the fallen men cautiously, his rifle trained on each body. They were all dead. It was over.

Meanwhile, Cassidy, her pistol drawn, edged toward the cabin. She moved with careful precision, her breath shallow as she approached the dark doorway. The cabin's interior was dark, acrid with the heavy stench of gunpowder. From the doorway, she scanned the room, her eyes darting over every shadow and crevice.

Suddenly, she froze, her body tensing as a gaze locked on to something inside. Then she stepped back toward the door. Her face paled, as she called out, "Quickly! Come and see this!"

CHAPTER FIFTY-SIX

The two boys were huddled in the corner of the dimly lit cabin, their ankles bound with thick ropes that tethered them to a heavy iron ring bolted to the wooden floor. They looked frightened, their faces pale and streaked with grime.

Grey had followed Cassidy into the dimly lit cabin, his sharp gaze sweeping the room before landing on the boys. His frown deepened. "It's the Hennessy Boys. They belong to the rancher who lives behind the general store," he said. "That family doesn't come into Nowhere often. They own a massive spread of land, but their ranch is closer to Duloe. I've been keeping an eye out since I heard they were missing, but I never imagined Buck would be behind it." Grey stepped closer, his jaw tightening. "It's Liam and Pat, isn't it?"

The two boys nodded their heads at this, the younger one clutching his brother's hand.

Meanwhile, Cassidy had crouched down beside the boys. Her movements were calm and deliberate as she began speaking to them in a soft, steady voice. "It's all right now. We have you safe and will return you to your parents." From beneath the folds of her skirt, she drew the large knife she always carried now, a trick she'd picked up from Amy. With practiced ease, she cut through the ropes and worked the tight knots loose from their ankles. The younger boy, overcome with relief, flung himself into her arms, sobbing uncontrollably. Cassidy held him close, murmuring soothing words as she glanced at the older boy, who was biting his lip in a valiant effort to hold back tears. He lasted only a moment longer before the floodgates opened, and Cassidy wrapped her arms around both boys, cradling them as if they were her own.

For several minutes, the cabin was filled with the boys' sobs. The release of the fear they must have endured for several days mingled with the quiet murmurs of Cassidy's reassurances. Grey stood nearby, his arms crossed, his expression hard to read.

It was some time before the boys were calm enough to speak. Outside, the light was already fading, and the day had advanced into late afternoon. The kidnappers' bodies had been buried beneath a cairn of rocks, because the frozen ground was too hard to dig proper graves. Grey, Sam and the two Indians had carried out the outdoor task, leaving Cassidy and Josh to tidy the cabin and prepare sleeping arrangements for the night.

Grey shook the snow off his boots as he re-entered the cabin. "We'll stay here until morning," Grey said, glancing out at the snow, which was falling again. "It's too dangerous to risk a journey to the cave with the boys in this weather, especially with night coming on."

"Where are Sam and the others?" Josh asked, looking up from the stove, where he was adding more wood.

Grey, pouring himself a cup of coffee from the pot Cassidy found brewed on the stove, replied, "Gone to join another group further up in Devil's Mountain."

The makeshift meal Cassidy and Josh prepared was simple and hot, if a bit peculiar, but no one complained. The boys, now sitting unshackled on a rug, devoured their food. Cassidy suspected they had seen little food during their captivity. The few provisions the group had brought had been cobbled together by Cassidy into a tasty stew with the supplies left behind by the kidnappers.

Grey leaned back against the wall near the stove, his

hand resting by the coffeepot. "Did Buck bring you back here when he took you?" he asked the boys. "You were on the ranch when he found you, weren't you?"

The older boy hesitated, then nodded. His voice was soft at first, but as he realized everyone was listening intently, he gained confidence and it grew stronger. "We were playing out back, near the ranch house. These two men came walking out from the trees. They'd left their horses farther back. I think they were watching the ranch for some time before they came up to us. Buck said he could hold us for ransom."

The boy paused, taking a shaky breath. Cassidy gave him an encouraging smile, and he continued. "They took us to a house in Duloe for a while. Then Buck told them to bring us up here. There were two of them, but they argued. The one that didn't want to go along with Buck's plan, he left us. We stayed here in this cabin with the other guy."

"Do you know what Buck planned to do after he got the ransom?" Grey's gaze sharpened.

The boy nodded, his hands fidgeting in his lap. "He said they were going to Mexico. Buck said they'd be rich there and could live like ..." He faltered, struggling to recall the exact words.

"Like kings?" Cassidy offered.

Relief flickered across the boy's face. "Yeah, like kings."

Grey's expression darkened, his face lined with anger. "Well, when the weather clears, we'll get you back to your parents," he said, his voice steady but grim.

Talk turned to the snow and how long it might last, but the conversation was interrupted when the younger boy, his voice soft but insistent, spoke up. "Don't you want to know where the gold is?"

The room fell silent. Grey's voice, low and edged with curiosity, broke the stillness. "Gold? Buck had gold?"

CHAPTER FIFTY-SEVEN

The boy nodded, casting anxious glances at each adult. "Yes. But you won't fight over it if I show you where it is, will you?"

Grey exchanged a look with the others before speaking. "We won't fight over it," he said firmly, his tone brooking no argument.

The boy seemed reassured. "Outside, there's a flat stone in front of a bank of grass and trees. I saw him hide it there one day."

Grey rose from his chair, gesturing for the boy to lead the way. "Show us." The group followed Liam to the cabin door. Snow had piled up in drifts, heavy and stubborn, against the threshold. Grey stepped in front of the boy, pushing his shoulder against the door, shoving it open with a groan against the weight of snow. They stepped out into the twilight, the snow falling in swirling flurries. Snow had piled up in drifts against the rocks and against the cabin itself.

"Can you remember where it was? Even under all the snow that's fallen?" Grey murmured to the boy as they stood in the doorway.

Liam nodded, determination flashing in his young eyes. Ignoring the swirling flurries of snow, Liam, a tiny figure in the deepening dusk, led them with no hesitation toward the edge of a small plateau. Snow crunched underfoot as the group trailed him toward the edge of the plateau. A jumble of rocks lay at the base of a bank of boulders. Their shape could be seen despite being covered in snow. Liam pointed to a largish flat stone leaning against the bank.

"That one," he said.

The others gathered around him, ignoring the snow falling on them, with Cassidy holding up an oil lamp.

"He pulled that flat stone back. The stuff is hidden behind it," Liam said again, pointing to the flat stone vanishing under a drift of snow.

"Shovels—we need shovels to move that snow," Josh said.

"I know where they are," Liam said and darted off to the side of the cabin, moments later reappearing with two large shovels. "Here, I got them."

"Thanks, Liam," Grey said, taking a shovel—but his gaze was intent on the stone. He and Josh, with a shovel each, soon shifted the snow.

Then Grey stooped. "Josh, help me shift this."

Josh knelt beside him and together they moved the stone aside, revealing a hidden hollow beneath. Inside were several bags and boxes. The group worked quickly, passing the items back to the boys and Cassidy to take back to the cabin. Once inside, they placed the cache on the rickety table, its surface groaning under the weight.

For a moment, no one spoke, each person staring at the hoard. The flickering firelight danced over the faces of the two boys, now watching with wide eyes, and the adults, who were all too aware of the implications of what they had found.

Grey finally broke the silence. "We'll deal with this later," he said, his tone uncompromising. "Tonight we sleep. Time enough to deal with it in the morning."

Grey woke them all before dawn, his voice cutting through a chill that had seeped into the cabin overnight. "Up and moving!" he called out. "I don't like this weather. There's no frost. If a storm rolls in, we'll have a devil's time getting down the mountain. Hard-packed snow and ice are bad enough, but melting snow? That's worse."

The group stirred reluctantly, pulling on boots and coats against the bitter wind. As the first rays of light stretched over the mountains, painting the snow in muted gold, they could see that the light was strange and unsettling, casting long shadows across the canyon.

Sam sniffed the air and frowned. "Doesn't feel right," he muttered, joining Grey to study the dawn creeping over the peaks. The two exchanged a glance that spoke volumes.

"If we're fast, we might not need to stop at the cave," Grey said, tightening the cinch on his saddle. "Best to head straight for Nowhere and Dry Creek Ranch."

The Hennessy boys were already saddling their horses. For their age, they were remarkably skilled horsemen. Despite the size and power of their mounts, they managed them with an ease that belied their youth. Grey nodded approvingly as he helped Liam onto his horse. "You ride well, son."

Liam grinned down at him, his cheeks red from the cold. "We help Pa round up cattle all the time. We've ridden all over the ranch."

That was the last bit of chatter for a while. No one looked back at the cabin; they were all eager to leave it behind. The descent down Devil's Mountain began in earnest. Here the snow lay thick in places, piled high in drifts that loomed against the cliffs and boulders. The horses navigated the narrow path with care, their breath steaming in the cold air. Each step crunched against the frozen ground, the sound echoing eerily in the canyon.

Grey had been right about the thaw. The snow was softening, and rivulets of meltwater trickled down the rocks. The heavy sky that had promised more snow was long gone, replaced by bright sunlight that lit their path and hastened the thaw.

"Should we stop for a break?" Josh asked Sam, whose gaze was fixed on the terrain ahead. He hesitated before nodding. "Let's ask Grey."

Sam rode forward, and Josh watched as he and Grey conferred in low voices. Though their words were lost to the wind, the grim set of Grey's face decision was clear. Grey's hand was raised, signalling a halt near a stream, the horses eagerly lowering their heads to drink. Sam and Grey exchanged uneasy glances as they noted the rising water level.

"It's a lot higher than when we came up," Sam observed.

"We don't have time for a fire or coffee," Grey said, his voice tight, his gaze fixed on the fast-flowing water. "The thaw's speeding up. If the sun keeps this up, the paths will turn into rivers of slush. And if it freezes tonight …" He trailed off, but the implication was clear.

Grey turned to the Hennessy boys. "Are you up for it? It'll be a long ride, but we'll go slow for the horses."

Liam sat tall in his saddle. "We can handle it," he said, though exhaustion was etched into their youthful faces. Their time in captivity had left them malnourished and frightened, but their frontier toughness shone through.

Grey's lips twitched into a brief smile before he turned his eyes back on the trailhead. "Then let's move."

CHAPTER FIFTY-EIGHT

By twilight, the shadows stretched long and deep across the foothills. The snow had turned into a steady drizzle, wet and relentless, soaking through coats as the group pushed forward. The trail, already treacherous, was now a mix of icy patches and thick, clinging mud.

Grey led the way, his shoulders hunched against the wind that whipped down the canyon behind him. "Keep together," Grey called over his shoulder, his voice barely carrying above the howling wind.

The trail widened, and the snow thinned, revealing patches of bare earth, still a treacherous mix of slush and ice. The sight of Nowhere, the scraggly beginnings of the township, brought a collective sigh of relief. Even the horses seemed to quicken their pace, sensing the end of the journey and the promise of warm stables.

Grey led them straight to the livery stable. Curly, the stable hand, appeared from the shadows, his surprise clear at their arrival. After a brief exchange, he sent a young boy riding to the Hennessy Ranch to deliver the news of the boys' rescue.

"Tell their parents they are staying with me in the hotel. They're too tired to make the journey tonight," Cassidy called out to the boy, and turned to the Hennessy lads. "Tonight, you sleep in the hotel. By morning, your parents will have arrived."

"We can't pay for a hotel, Miss. We got no money," Liam said. His face, drawn with exhaustion, now looked worried.

"Don't worry about the bill. You'll be staying with me," Cassidy assured them. She watched as Sam, Grey and Josh gathered the heavy bags of ill-gotten gains together. There had only been time that previous night to glance through the sacks of coins and jewellery the bandit had amassed. Grey was taking it all to the sheriff's office to sort out and look for details of the stolen goods, so that he might return them. What he would do if no owner could be found was something they were all wondering. But no one said anything. You didn't question sheriff Lance Grey's actions. If you did, you might not live to tell the tale.

"Cassidy, you'll be heading to the hotel with the boys," Grey said. "Josh, I expect you'll join them at the general store. Sam, you're welcome to bunk at the sheriff's office with me. After we've all washed and eaten something and had a good night's sleep, we'll get together to talk things through tomorrow morning."

Murmurs of agreement from the weary travelers greeted Grey's proposal. The Hennessy boys were tired. Eager to see their parents were also overwhelmed at the thought of spending a night in a hotel.

Leaving the horses in Curly's safe hands, they all walked together in a group toward the livery stable doors. Cassidy and Josh stood near the stable entrance, talking quietly. An icicle broke loose from the roof, crashing to the ground with a sharp crack.

"Look out everyone, icicles crashing down!" Sam shouted, the first to see the danger.

They all jumped back, startled. But, being nearest the door, Josh slipped on a patch of ice. His arms flailed wildly about as he grabbed for the stable door, but it was too late. His feet slid out from under him and he hit the ground hard. Josh found nothing to grab onto and fell heavily, his head striking the doorframe with a sickening thud.

Cassidy and Grey were at his side in an instant. "Josh, are you all right?" Cassidy's voice trembled.

Josh seemed to be unconscious, but after a moment, his eyes flickered open.

Grey eased Josh upright, his fingers exploring the back of his head. "You've got a nasty bump," he said. Josh groaned, his hand moving to his temple. "My head hurts …"

"Take it easy Josh," Sam said, offering him a canteen. Josh sipped the water slowly, his eyes darting around, as if trying to piece things together.

"That was quite a blow Josh. You fell heavily," Grey said, kneeling beside him.

Josh looked at Grey, and then around the stable yard and his gaze sharpened, and he stiffened. "Who … who's Josh? And who are you? What happened?"

A stunned silence fell over the others standing around Josh.

Cassidy's face paled, and she knelt down beside him. "Josh, it's me. Cassidy. Don't you remember anything?"

Josh's eyes darted between them, from one to the other, his confusion deepening. "I don't know any of you. Where am I?"

Cassidy's voice was barely a whisper. "He doesn't know who he is."

Josh's gaze shifted to Grey. "Who are you? What's happening to me?"

The silence that followed was unbroken for some time. No one knew what to say. Somewhere in the distance, a horse whinnied, its cry echoing through the night. A dog barked far away, and a couple of drunks leaving the saloon could be heard laughing uproariously.

But those in the livery stable stood frozen, their relief

at reaching safety now overshadowed by this unexpected turn of events.

What would Josh remember now?

About The Author

Janey Clarke writes charming, witty, cosy mysteries. From septuagenarian shenanigans in Cornwall to the intrigue of Regency-era whodunits and now to her newest venture into the rugged drama of the Wild West. When not plotting her next twist or researching historical details, she can be found exploring the stunning Jurassic Coast in Dorset with her loyal spaniel by her side. With a passion for tea, old books, and well-timed humor, Janey Clarke creates stories she hopes will whisk readers away to delightful worlds where solving a mystery is always the order of the day. And always solved by a feisty heroine!

Visit Janey at www.janeyclarke.com to learn more about her books.

www.blossomspringpublishing.com